I0599659

Copyright Page

The Draoidh's Gambit

© [2025] [Joseph L Wiess]

For permission requests, write to the publisher at: [Golden Plains Press]

[JosephWiess@gmail.com]

ISBN: [979-8-9934166-5-6]

Cover Design: [Joseph L Wiess]

Dedication

To my family: love you all.

To my dad: May God Grant you rest.

To my Employers: Thank you for allowing me
to play while at work.

Contents

Chapter One

The Mooring of the Dawn-Breaker

The clouds thinned around them as the Dawn Breaker descended, her hull groaning like an old tree bending before a storm. Veils of vapor curled away from her sails, trailing streamers of silver that clung to the rigging as if reluctant to let go. The sky still cradled them, offering freedom of movement, but the earth below pulled with its heavier promise, safety of hearth, safety of home.

The hundred-and-fifty-foot galleon steadied her fall as the heavens gave way to bright air. At her prow, the draoidh bent over the scrying orb, its surface clouded with pale light that swam and reformed into the terrain below.

The glass throbbed faintly beneath his hand, each beat like the pulse of the land itself.

"How does it look?" Marcus inquired as he stepped up behind his friend.

Rhyslin straightened, the faint sheen of prana still lingering in his eyes. "It looks like home," he replied with a smile, and for a heartbeat the orb glimmered brighter, as if affirming his words.

The ranger nodded, stretching his arms with a ripple of muscle and leather, his joints cracking like old branches. "I can't wait to be on solid ground." He would have leapt from the ship and walked the leagues barefoot if given half the chance.

Rhyslin understood well enough.

Though he loved the sweep of sky beneath the keel, there were times he longed for the simple rustle of leaves overhead and the loam beneath his boots. "We've only been airborne for a week," he teased.

"A week there, three weeks aground, and two weeks back. I miss the feel of dirt under my feet." The ranger leaned slightly over the prow, his cloak tugged by the wind. Below, the land rippled with shadow and light, far too distant for mercy.

"Don't fall overboard," Rhyslin warned, eyes glinting. "We're still high up. You'd make a wonderful splat on the ground."

Marcus squinted down at the dizzying height, then grunted. "I guess I'll just have to wait a bit. I guess now's a good time to tell you something."

When Rhyslin arched a brow, the ranger's voice grew solemn, steady as bedrock. "If anything untoward happens to me, you get Nat and the kids."

Rhyslin stared at Marcus, aghast, hand rising instinctively to his chest as if to ward off the enormity of the words. "You are, without a doubt, the strangest person I've ever met. Imagine a man so twisted that he would hand his wife and children —"

Marcus interrupted, the humor in his eyes breaking the solemn air. "And Saorshealbh."

"His wife, children, and his saorshealbh—"

"Don't forget my pack."

"Yes, yes, and your pack," Rhyslin echoed, shaking his head. Then he paused, truly considering.

"Your pack would follow me?" His gaze sharpened, measuring Marcus with sudden seriousness.

Marcus nodded once. "You are Mathair Astinmah's son," he said simply, as if that were the only proof required.

4

"Or so she keeps telling me," Rhyslin muttered, half bitter, half amused. Then his tone dropped, threading with a darker resonance. "You know, I may not live past tonight. Then it would be you inheriting my bonds and property."

"You're full of it," the ranger said, laughter spilling into the wind. "Here's what I think will happen." He waited until the draoidh turned that storm-colored glare upon him. "I think your Flur and Ria requested Daes-ghath-a-chaid dioladh and will talk with your seer for several hours before bringing her to you for binding."

Rhyslin's mouth tightened. "You think all that will happen, do you? That is very specific for a hunch." His fingers traced a lazy rune in the air, prana answering faintly in the rigging before fading, drawing a chortle from the ranger.

"I may have overheard them discussing it the other day."

"I thought as much," Rhyslin smirked. Silence fell, but it was not empty; the air trembled with the faint whirr of unseen wings, the rigging of the Dawn Breaker creaking as though the ship itself leaned in to listen. The orb at the prow pulsed once, like a heart responding to the cadence of their thoughts. At length, Rhyslin asked carefully, "Do you think Despoina will—?"

"Tell Rowena step by step how to get what she wants," Marcus said with a shrug. "She'll know exactly what to do."

Rhyslin's jaw tightened. The protest formed in his throat but withered; Marcus would only counter with the same truth he always carried—that Astinmah called Rhyslin son.

The weight of divine expectation pressed across his shoulders like the yardarm above his head, heavier than timber or rope. He turned back to the horizon, frowning, as the light dimmed behind a gauze of passing cloud.

"A sgillin for your thoughts," Marcus grinned, as if reading the current beneath Rhyslin's silence.

"Just thinking about the gods and their taghta." Rhyslin shrugged, not even sparing a glance. The word carried on the wind like a bell tolling at a funeral, hollow and sure.

When the ranger grunted, Rhyslin muttered under his breath. "Go ahead and say it."

"Nope, got nothing to say."

"Really?" Rhyslin blinked when Marcus only nodded. "That's a first. Usually, I can't get you to shut up."

The ranger's grin widened, sly as a fox basking in firelight.

Rhyslin shook his head, exasperated.

"Since each god has a taghta," Marcus teased, "does that mean you are a' Mathair's taghta?"

"Not on your life," Rhyslin shook with mirth. His laugh rolled low, but the smile that followed was laced with weariness. "I know her too well to be a true disciple." His gaze drifted, shadows etching deeper across his brow.

"I would probably drive her believers away if I told them the truth about her." He knew, even as he said it, that they'd never go that far.

"What truth would that be?" Marcus looked at the draoidh, eyes narrowing with the kind of curiosity that smelled faintly of danger.

Rather than answer, Rhyslin leaned lazily against the rail, his expression sliding toward boredom. The wind tugged at his cloak, whispering as if eager to spill what he would not. "What do all women want, even if they deny it?"

Marcus glanced at his friend, uncertain where this road would lead. "A strong man, a home, a family, love, and protection." The words left his mouth by rote, worn smooth by generations.

The draoidh confirmed them with a rhetorical question, his voice weighted like a stone dropped into still water.

"Can it be any different for a goddess?"

The ranger blinked, shocked. "Truly?"

Rhyslin nodded somberly. Even the sails overhead stilled in the lull, as though the ship itself leaned closer to the confession.

"He who watches created this world as a refuge for a' Mathair after her gardens were all destroyed on the world that was."

He paused just as the women drew near, their steps soft on the deck, the air shifting with the scent of resin and sky-salt. "Mathair Astinmah is not a creator goddess." His eyes swept across them, gauging the weight of his words as silence pressed heavy as fog. "A' Mathair is a nurturing goddess."

When Rana looked skeptical, Rhyslin continued, his tone gentling like rainfall through leaves. "She loves wild growing places; she surrounds herself with Dryads and nature spirits. She doesn't want to fight and has welcomed refugees from other worlds and planes."

He glanced at Marcus, who nodded, leaning against his staff with a faint creak of wood against wood.

"A' Mathair doesn't want to rule," he added with a snort. Natolie's chuckle broke the tension like kindling snapping in a fire. Rhyslin's voice dropped, mournful now. "Why do you think she keeps trying to give me that horrible crown?"

The lake stretched wide below them, a mirror of still steel beneath the Dawn Breaker's keel.

The air smelled faintly of damp iron and pine, touched with the resinous sharpness of dockside forests.

"I wondered about that," Marcus admitted, then looked away as O'Cuire raised a hand to signal the crew. "I think it's about time."

"Time for what?" Rana asked the ranger, her eyes bright with eagerness.

"To hit the water," Marcus said with a grin.

Rhyslin shook his head, the wind teasing strands of his pale hair. "Not this time. That creature did enough damage to the hull that a water landing might sink her."

Marcus winced, breath hitching as memory clawed up—the void monster, its maw tearing into planks, two crewmen vanishing with only a scream. "By Nan Diathan, I forgot about that."

Rhyslin arched his left brow, a shadow of humor covering the steel in his gaze. "You're getting forgetful in your old age." He tried to make it a jest, though the ship beneath their feet still bore scars.

Marcus leaned against the rail, the wood creaking in sympathy. "Just you wait, young man. One day it'll be you who's forgetting things."

Rana, thrumming with energy like a bowstring drawn too long, waited until the two men were through their sparring.

"If you aren't landing in water, where are you going to dock?"

"The drydock," Rhyslin said simply, his voice carrying the weight of decision as his eyes followed the ship's captain.

O'Cuire stood with the practiced calm of command, gaze sweeping upward as the lower sails were furled and lashed to the yardarms. Canvas rippled like sighing ghosts, the Dawn Breaker easing into a slow hover over the cradle prepared for her.

"Andros, let me know when we are in position."

The earth elemental knelt on the deck, his fingers splaying across the planks as though the ship's bones were his own. Closing his eyes, he reached downward with his senses, threads of earthen resonance finding the cold iron blocks below. The timbers hummed faintly beneath his touch.

He waited until the vessel's heart aligned with the cradle's, then opened his eyes. "Now, sir."

The captain drew his right hand to his chest. Along the yards, the topsails fell into place with a sound like wings folding, the ship's forward thrust dwindling into stillness. Hovering now, twenty feet above the lake's glassy skin, she seemed to breathe.

O'Cuire glanced at Andros again, and when the elemental gave a steady nod, the captain signaled. Fore and aft anchors uncoiled with a thunder of links, the heavy cables plunging toward earth.

Rana darted to the rail, hair flying, leaning over just far enough to glimpse the world below. The air rose cool and empty, the anchors vanishing into shadow.

She studied the process with fascination as the deck crew barked orders and secured equipment. "Are they not using the capstan?"

She stumbled slightly over the word, self-conscious.

"No, the capstan isn't needed." Rhyslin's eyes narrowed, catching something in her tone. "What did you see when you looked down?"

Rana answered quickly, too quickly. "Nothing. What was I supposed to see?" Her pulse thrummed like the taut rigging overhead, her whole body alive with restless, questioning energy.

The Dawn Breaker groaned faintly beneath their feet, as if she too was waiting for an answer.

"You'll see in a minute," Rhyslin commented, his gaze flicking toward Andros. "Andros, are they down there?"

Out of the corner of his eye, he caught Flur and Ria at the rail, hair stirring in the wind, bracing themselves with the ease of women long accustomed to flight.

He was about to warn Rana when he noticed her knees bend, balance sure as a sailor's. Instead of reaching for the railing, she crossed the deck in three light steps, took his staff just below his hand, and spun in a graceful half-turn until she was pressed back against him, her body settling with startling familiarity into the curve of his.

Rhyslin arched a brow as she drew his right hand across her abdomen, anchoring herself in his touch.

"Am I suddenly the most secure thing on the deck?" His fingers spread across the dome of her belly, feeling the warmth of life beneath, the rise and fall of her breath.

Rana nodded, cheeks flushed pink, the tips of her ears burning. She tilted her head up, her green eyes vivid against her dusky skin, her aquiline nose catching the slant of light. Her lips curled in a grin both impudent and shy.

The draoidh studied her profile, the way youth and fire mingled there. She rocked her hips back, brushing across his manhood with deliberate mischief.

"If you don't stop that," he warned, voice deepening, "you're going to get into trouble."

His attempt to keep from responding to her, failed as her grin sharpened into a devious smile, and she pressed harder, playful defiance in every movement.

His tone cut low, steel wrapped in velvet. "If you don't stop this, I will take you over my knees and tan your hide."

Beneath his palm her belly tightened, then shivered as though a storm passed through her. Rana froze, lips parting into a perfect O, a sound spilling soft as prayer.

More shivers coursed through her frame, trembling beneath his fingers. That sealed it, truth unveiled.

She was submissive, her soul yielding as naturally as breath. Rhyslin closed his eyes and prayed to Mathair Astinmah for patience, the goddess' silence pressing back upon him like the sea against a hull.

Before the moment could deepen, the timbers of the dock boomed. A shadow fell across the ship as the first iron golem stepped into view. Fifteen feet tall, its metallic frame gleamed, runes pulsing faintly across bronze-like plates. It halted at sight of Rhyslin, then raised an arm in solemn greeting.

Rana gasped, pointing excitedly. "What is that?"

"It's an iron golem."

The massive construct's gesture echoed with the scrape of metal on metal. Rhyslin inclined his head in return, acknowledging the ancient thing as one master to another.

Seconds later, the ground trembled as the second golem appeared, each step landing with the weight of thunder.

The Dawn Breaker eased into the cradle's embrace, the air alive with the smell of heated iron and the creak of straining timbers as she was secured.

Rhyslin caught the captain's attention with a measured glance, the weight of command pressing in the air.

"I'll be in my office. Let me know when the men are off-loaded and ready to leave."

The timber of his voice carried through the planks like a drumbeat, and the captain dipped his head in assent. Only then did Rhyslin turn, cloak stirring faintly as though drawn by a hidden current, and stride back into his office.

The room was cooler, shadows wrapped close by the tall bookshelves, the faint tang of ink and leather softening the air.

Ria, Flur, and Rana trailed behind him, their presence folding into the space like threads woven through a tapestry.

"Do you mind going and packing our things?" Rhyslin asked, turning toward Flur.

"Of course not, maighstir." Her voice was warm as a hearthfire, and she brushed a kiss to his cheek, a spark of light in the dim chamber.

Then she caught Rana's hand, tugging her with a playful urgency, skirts whispering as they slipped out. The door hushed closed, and silence returned like a waiting breath.

Left alone, Ria's fingers toyed with the folds of her skirt. The air shifted with her hesitation, a fragile flutter like leaves stirred in a half-wind. "What can I do, Maighstir?" Her green eyes flickered from him to the bookshelf, then back again, restless.

"Help me find a leather-bound book with a green spine." His voice was muffled, head bent into a drawer, the rasp of papers and wood filling the pause. "I know I had that book when we left the manse."

Ria moved toward the shelves, fingertips grazing the spines as though the books might whisper their secrets. She thought, with a twist in her chest, that Rhyslin had more volumes here than she had owned in her entire household.

Then, a flash of green. She drew the book gently, reverently, holding it aloft. "Is this the one?"

The Draoidh looked up from the box by his desk. "Yes, that's the one. You're a gem."

The praise lit her cheeks in a slow-burning blush, warmth that pulsed down into her chest.

She beamed despite herself, and the very boards beneath her feet seemed to hum with the shared spark.

"What's so important about this book?" She held it toward him, offering.

"Take a look and see if you can figure it out." He leaned back, gaze steady, inviting.

She laid the book on the desk and opened it with care. The scent of ink and parchment drifted up like a memory. Her eyes flickered across elegant script, the names breathing like ghosts from the page. "It's a ledger, isn't it?" She glanced up, catching the tilt of his nod. "But it's not a general ledger."

Her finger traced a line like a pilgrim along a prayer-bead. "Lieutenant Isom Istare, commander of the Blackguards, Forty-nine soldiers." Her hand trembled faintly as she turned another page.

"Ranger Commander Marcus Tanner, Natolie Tanner, Twenty-five Ranger scouts, twenty-four Infernal soldiers."

Her voice softened as she touched another line. "Sergeant Torval—" The name flared across her cheeks, a betraying blush. "Twenty soldiers, 1 cannon crew, four Magaidhean." She looked up, breath quickening. "It's a paybook, isn't it?"

"That it is." Rhyslin's grin broke the tension, a warm light through a storm cloud. "And before we can go to the manse, we must fix one small thing."

When she arched a brow, he continued, "The original contract was for three weeks, and thanks to Mathair's meddling, my three-day sleep, and the weeks of travel back, I owe them three extra weeks pay."

He leaned back, stretching, the wood of his chair creaking like old trees in wind. "Do you see the bundles of square tickets?"

She nodded, eyes finding them.

"Each of those bundles goes to the captains of the squads. We must add three extra ticks to each ticket and then get them to each captain before they can dismiss their men."

Ria calculated silently, lips pursing, the quill and ink already shaping themselves in her imagination. "I can get them done in two hours," she admitted, concern touching her tone. "Is it fair to make them stand out in the sun that long?"

"No, it's not." Rhyslin's voice gentled, the air itself easing. "Since it's my fault they got delayed, I'll take half of those. That should cut it down to an hour."

She pulled two of the four bundles and handed them across the desk. His hand brushed hers as he gave her quill and ink, a fleeting spark that left her pulse unsteady.

"May we help, maighstir?"

24

Both looked up to see Flur and Rana hovering in the doorway, the light from the hall framing them like figures in a painted triptych.

"It'll go quicker if you have more hands." Flur's tone was lilting; Rana's gaze steady as iron.

Rhyslin studied them for a breath, then nodded. "Very well. Grab a stack and add three ticks to each ticket. You don't have to do this."

"We know, Maighstir, but we want to." Rana's voice cut firm, certain, as she took a quill and settled beside Ria.

Together they bent over the desk, four pairs of hands scratching ink across parchment. The sound was steady, almost ritualistic, like prayer chimes ringing in unison. With every tick, time compressed, labor transformed into intimacy.

After forty-five minutes, Rana set down her quill with a flourish. "Done!" She wiped it clean and placed it in Rhyslin's hand. "Now what?"

"I want each of you to take a stack of tickets and find a captain," Rhyslin said, gathering his. "I'll take these to Marcus."

"No, you won't."

Keisha breezed through the doorway, her presence carrying the crisp scent of green wood. "I'll take those and find Maighstir Marcus." She plucked the stack from his hand with dryad quickness.

When he frowned, she only laughed, sticking out her tongue before darting away, laughter echoing down the hall.

"I'll go find Torval," Ria murmured, clutching her bundle. She slipped away quietly, the echo of her footsteps like a heartbeat receding.

Rana glanced down at her stack. "I'll go find Lieutenant Istare." Before Rhyslin could guide her, she had already vanished into the corridor.

Flur lingered, reading her slip. "That leaves me with Captain K'Tek." Her brow furrowed briefly. "That's the Infernal that signed the accords, right?"

When Rhyslin nodded, she smiled. "I think I saw him with some of his men at the gangplank."

She leaned down, unable to resist, lips brushing his in a quick kiss that tasted of daring. "I'll be back shortly, Maighstir," she whispered, and with a wink she was gone, skirt swaying like a flame caught in wind.

The office fell quiet again, charged with the fading echoes of their footsteps and laughter, the hush of duty completed, intimacy left hanging in the air.

Rhyslin stared at the door long after it closed, his thoughts scattered like leaves in a restless wind. He had gone from solitude to being surrounded by four women, with the promise of yet another to come. The weight of it pressed against him—not crushing, but disorienting. He pushed back from the desk and rose slowly, as if standing might steady his mind.

From somewhere in the rafters of the world, laughter rippled across the air. He tilted his head, lips curling despite himself. "Of course, you'd think this is funny," he muttered. His voice was softer now, reverent in its weariness. "But despite your sense of humor, I do love you, Mathair."

The laughter faded, leaving behind a hush so tender it stirred the fine hairs at his temple.

He could almost swear he felt fingers stroke across his scalp, mother-gentle, reminding him he was never as alone as he sometimes feared.

By the time he stepped out onto the quarterdeck, the air itself had changed. Two hundred soldiers stood at attention, their stillness pressing like a living wall. Their captains and lieutenants flanked them, a row of steel and discipline.

Even the wind seemed to hold its breath, carrying only the creak of timbers and the faint scent of iron and sweat.

When Rhyslin appeared, the line of warriors moved as one. Each fist pressed over the heart, each arm extended outward to open palm. The gesture shimmered with unspoken oath.

The draoidh returned their salute, his fingers cutting through the air as he traced a rune that flared briefly, bright as dawnfire. His voice carried, filling not just ears but chests, until the deck itself seemed to resonate with his words.

"Soldiers of the Saor-shealbhaidhean, I want to thank you for all you've done."

A thunder of cheers broke loose, a storm of joy held just barely in check.

He waited, patient as stone, until the waves ebbed.

"It is a testament to your training, your honor, and your determination that you defeated an army almost twice your size."

The cheers rose again, mingled with whoops that carried the relief of survivors. Somewhere in the crowd, steel boots stamped in time with the cries, grounding the noise in rhythm.

When at last silence reclaimed the space, Rhyslin's gaze swept the ranks. It felt, to each soldier, as though his eyes had lingered on them alone. Such was the draoidh's gift—and his burden.

"I am deeply indebted that you chose to stay near me while I was unconscious and acted as the protectors of the Hin I-Balanath. You could have easily returned to your homes and been here sooner."

The murmured refusals came low, a tide of voices pushing back against the thought, carrying with them the taste of iron loyalty.

"You have acted beyond the scope of your contract," Rhyslin continued, his tone firm now, ritual-deep. "And because you did so, I am going to add three weeks to your contract and pay you for those weeks."

He reached into his pocket and drew out a ticket. The square slip gleamed faintly, ink and promise woven together.

"Each of you should have your pay stub."

Hands lifted, a few stubs raised toward the waning light as if in silent offering.

"Thank you from the bottom of my heart. You can start cashing in the paystubs tomorrow morning after sunrise. Until then, enjoy the night with your families and friends."

This time, he raised his arm first, fist to heart, hand opening like a blessing. The salute rippled outward, mirrored by two hundred strong, until the entire quarterdeck throbbed with a single heartbeat of loyalty.

The captains' voices cracked like thunder, "Dismissed!" followed by the sergeants echoing the command, their words scattering the formation like sparks across dry wood.

The soldiers broke apart, laughter and relief rising into the evening air, carried on the wind that still smelled faintly of runes and reverence.

Chapter Two
The Bathhouse of Quiet Waters

It was mid-afternoon when the men
dispersed to seek their families. Rhyslin
lingered at the rail until the quarterdeck had
nearly emptied. Only then did he descend
toward the gangplank, where the four women
gathered around him like quiet
constellations.

Keisha skipped ahead, her laughter light
as wind over leaves, and jabbed his arm with
a fingertip. "Are you gonna face down the
seer?"

Rhyslin shook his head. "No, I'm going
to bathe." When she poked again, he caught
her finger and held it still. "Flur and Ria have
asked to perform Deas-ghnàth a' chiad
diùltadh, and I've allowed it."

His chest rose with a steady breath before he turned to Rana. "Are you still going to join me?"

The young spell-blade flushed, but instead of retreating she lifted her chin with a sudden spark of pride. "Yes, maighstir, I am. You still have to prove to me that you have that bathhouse."

His answering grin matched hers, and together they turned up the path toward the manor.

"What about our luggage?" Ria asked, halting him with a raised hand. "Do we just leave it here?"

"Of course not," Rhyslin said. "You can either carry it or wait a few minutes for the automata to fetch it."

The three women gave him a level stare that tugged a chuckle out of him. "I didn't tell you about the automata, did I?"

"No, maighstir mo ghràidh, you didn't," Flur replied, glancing to Ria, who merely shrugged.

"The dockhands who moored the ship were their larger kin," he explained. "Their smaller cousins carry burdens, mend walls, and lend their strength to whatever task is needed."

Even as he spoke, the earth at the foot of the hill stirred, and five stone-wrought figures climbed free of the soil with ponderous care.

"Here they are now." Rhyslin gestured to the foremost. "Please take the luggage to the manor and set it in the foyer."

The stone men bent with surprising gentleness, lifted each trunk as if it were no heavier than a branch, and marched uphill toward the house. The air hummed faintly with the echo of their inner cores—an old craft Rhyslin had bound into the land long ago.

"If you follow me, I'll lead you to the foyer. From there, a servant will take you two —" he nodded toward Flur and Ria, "to my office, where I think Rowena will be waiting."

His gaze slid to Rana, warm with amusement. "Our intrepid spell-blade and I will find the bathhouse and wash the dust of travel from our bones."

"What should I do, Maighstir?" Keisha asked, half-skipping to keep up with his stride.

"Find Matron Foghar," Rhyslin answered without hesitation. "Ask her if she's willing to train you for what lies ahead."

The dryad bit her lip, abashed, but she darted forward to wrap him in a brief, fierce hug before racing toward the grove. The green around her seemed to sigh in approval as she vanished into the trees.

The three who remained fell in step behind Rhyslin. The path wound through flowerbeds and young groves, every plant alive with the slow pulse of his decades of tending. The scent of loam and blossom mingled in the air, calming and thick as incense.

"It's so beautiful," Flur whispered, as though louder words might disturb the place. She bent to breathe the fragrance of a blue-petaled bloom, her voice reverent. "It must have taken you years to create this."

"It did," Rhyslin admitted. "Decades, to shape it as I wished. Every blade, every branch serves a purpose." The grass beneath their feet answered faintly as he spoke, bending toward his presence.

Rana crouched and pressed her palm flat to the path. "What is this made from? It gives and flexes."

"Ground tree bark, packed earth, and mulched grass," he replied. "I wanted something that could endure heavy tread and still belong to the living land." He tapped the butt of his stave against the walkway, and the ground seemed to answer with a subtle tone. "I haven't had to do more than minor repairs in twenty years."

"That's amazing." Rana rose, eyes half-closed, her breath drawn deep as if the place itself poured into her. "It smells good here."

She turned slowly, drinking in the color and the air, her stance loosening as though she might one day belong to this soil.

Rhyslin watched, a secret smile curving his lips, and turned his head toward the horizon. He had been listening for it, and when the three Hin I-Balanath lifted their eyes as one, he knew they had heard it too: a thin, bright cry on the eastern wind.

Ria and Flur shaded their eyes with mirrored gestures. Rana's hand fell instinctively to the hilt of her sword as she edged closer to Rhyslin, her body braced against the unseen call.

"Rhyyyyyyspeeeeeet!"

The cry cut the sky like silver thread. Rhyslin lifted his head as a blur of wings streaked down, scattering petals from the flowerbeds.

The air hummed with her passage, a bright, fey pitch that made the grass quiver and the blossoms tremble.

"It is you. You're back."

The fairy squealed as she flung herself against him, burrowing into his hair near his ear. Tiny wings beat against his cheek; the faint scent of nectar and wild clover clung to her. "I've missed you so much, Rhyspet." She crooned, pressing quick, dew-light kisses against his earlobe.

"I've missed you too, Kita." Rhyslin's voice softened as he reached up, offering his palm. The small woman wriggled free of his hair, fluttered once, and settled into his hand. Her joy lit her features like dawn, and the weight of her presence made the air feel sharper, livelier.

The three Hin I-Balanath women leaned closer, curiosity stirring the green around them. Leaves shifted toward the fairy as if the land itself bent to her brightness. Kita spun, eyes wide.

"Oooooh, you brought new people with you."

She zipped upward, circling Flur's head, tugging at golden strands that glimmered like sunlit grain. "Oh, such pretty golden hair. What's your name?"

"Flur," the bhanna replied with a faint smile tugging at her lips. "And who are you?"

"Kita," the fairy sang, alighting on Flur's shoulder. "Ohhh, you're bonded to Rhyspet, I can tell."

Before Flur could reply, she darted to Ria, wings stirring the air like a harp's high string. "I love your eyes; they are such a pretty green."

When Ria extended her hand, Kita perched in her palm and peered up with scrunched delight.

"I am Ria," she said warmly. "I'm also bonded to Rhyslin." With a glance, she gestured toward Rana. "This is my daughter, Rana."

"Hello, Ranapet." Kita waved merrily. "You're not bonded." Her tone carried neither judgment nor pity, only fact. She turned at once and zipped back to Rhyslin. Her expression faltered, small brow knitting. "Wena's not going to be happy."

The concern in her tiny voice was sharp as birdsong. "Do you need me to go with you?"

Rhyslin chuckled, the sound grounding the moment. "No, not unless you want to go to the bathhouse with me."

Kita tilted her head, wings whispering. "If you aren't going to see Wena, who is?" Her worry hung in the air like a faint tremor, tugging at even the flowers.

"Ria and Flur will talk to Rowena first," the draoidh assured her.

At that, Kita spun back to Ria's waiting hand, joy returning. "I can go with you, yes?"

When Ria nodded, Kita's laugh rang bright. "Can't wait to see what Wena does when she sees you."

She scampered up Ria's arm and vanished beneath her hair near her ear, her wings buzzing softly like a secret hidden in the leaves.

"See you later, Rhyspet."

"Fly free, Kita," Rhyslin said with a smile. He lingered a moment, watching the fairy lead Flur and Ria up the path toward the door, before turning aside. The air felt lighter in her wake, though the mention of Rowena pressed like a shadow on his thoughts.

Rhyslin hummed low in his chest as he stepped off the path, the sound carrying like a deep note through the meadow. He bent, unlaced his boots, and set them aside.

A smile softened his face as he spread his toes in the grass. The earth answered at once, warmth seeping up through soil and root, threads of life tugging back into his being.

Rana watched, eyes wide, as though afraid to blink and miss some hidden ritual.

When Rhyslin closed his eyes, posture settling into a rare ease, the air itself hushed.

A bird trilled once in the branches and then fell silent, listening.

She hesitated only a moment before following suit, pulling free her boots and sinking to her knees in the grass. Pressing both palms flat, she giggled softly when a beetle clambered across her skin, its tiny weight a tickling benediction.

When she lifted her gaze again, Rhyslin was seated beside her, his presence steady as stone.

"How much can you feel?" He gestured lightly to the land around them.

Rana worried her lower lip, searching for words. "Almost everything. I can feel the flowers reaching for the sun. I can feel the trees and grass, and I can feel some of the animals."

She tilted her head toward the tall willow whose branches brushed the ground.

Her brow quirked. "Why does that one feel so odd?"

Rhyslin followed her glance, closing his eyes again. For a moment his breathing matched the sway of leaves. "I see. That's a Seileach tree, and for as long as I've been here, the Dryad inside has been asleep. I keep hoping she'll wake, but she's content to sleep."

The young spellblade reached over and caught his hand. Her fingers were warm against his, her voice quieter. "Maybe she feels safe, so she doesn't need to be awake." She traced the lines of his palm with reverence, almost as though reading runes written into his skin. "I understand how she feels."

"Oh? How's that?" He curled his fingers lightly around hers, anchoring the touch.

A playful smile tugged at her lips. "From the moment I boarded your ship, I felt safe."

She edged closer, grass bending beneath her knees. "I've slept better than I have for eight years."

When he did not move to stop her, Rana slipped into his lap, her head finding his shoulder as if it belonged there. Yet simple nearness was not enough; a whimper escaped her throat—fragile, seeking.

Rhyslin's arms came around her at once, closing her in. At that, her whole body melted, settling against him, as if the earth itself had exhaled in relief.

So still were they in that embrace that neither noticed the tree stir. The bark of the Seileach whispered apart, forming a doorway, and a fox-eared dryad peeked through.

Gold eyes gleamed beneath the sweep of willow-shadow. She watched the pair a long moment, tail swishing once in faint approval, before retreating back into her tree.

Chapter Three
Smoke and Silence in the Study

At the same time Rhyslin and Rana were sitting under the Willow tree, Flur and Ria followed Kita's directions as they made their way up the path to the manse.

For once, Kita wasn't babbling needlessly. The silence pressed in around them like damp wool, broken only by the crunch of gravel beneath their feet. Flur noticed how the fairy's wings gave off a faint, restless shimmer of light, dimmer than usual.

She couldn't decide whether it was because of the two Hin I-Balanath or because they would soon speak to the seeress, and Kita longed to be there for that.

Upon arriving at the front door, Kita mumbled, "It's not locked. You can go right in.

The words hung in the air with a metallic taste, as if the threshold itself disapproved of their arrival.

Flur paused and looked to Ria—or more accurately, to the shimmer of air where she knew the fairy rode. "What's wrong, Kita?"

"Nothing," Kita prevaricated. "It's just that I don't get along very well with Wena."

The golden-haired bhanna's blue eyes narrowed slightly. She had the sense that Kita was hiding something, though whatever it was, it did not strike her as life-threatening. Still, the air prickled faintly along her arms, carrying the dry scent of sage and iron. With a shrug, she reached out and pushed the door open.

"Hello?" she called out as she stepped into the foyer.

"Is anyone here?"

When there was no answer, she took time to look around. The entryway was circular, its high walls echoing faintly with her voice. Potted plants circled the room, their leaves trembling faintly as if stirred by an unseen current.

The air was cool and green, touched with the earthy scent of moss and wet clay. On the walls hung paintings of ponds and groves, each framed in wood that seemed to pulse faintly with life.

"He has good taste, that's for sure," Ria whispered as she looked around. "He's creating a quiet space that invites you inside."

The hin- i-balalanth matron commented softly, her words laced with the faint hum of agreement from the room itself. She glanced around. "You'd think someone would be waiting here, especially if they know the Maighstir is back."

Flur brushed her fingers through her hair, her eyes narrowing slightly in confusion. "Do you think there's some way to let them know we are here?"

"Oh, they know we are here," Kita groused. The air near her shimmered like disturbed water. "They just feel as if they don't have to answer to anyone but Rhyspet." Ria could tell that the treatment miffed the fairy.

"Do they treat every guest this way?" Flur inquired, noticing a bell rope hanging near the opposite door, which she figured led into the rest of the house.

The fairy shook her head. "No, just women, and so far, Rhyspet hasn't corrected them."

Flur glanced at Ria, who shrugged, then marched over to the rope and gave it a sharp tug. The bell rang, its tone carrying a sharp shiver through the plants.

A young woman appeared, her steps quick, eyes downcast. "Welcome home," she started, then examined Flur and Ria from head to foot. "You aren't Maighstir Rhyslin. Who are you?"

Flur drew herself to her full height and tossed her hair back. "I am Flur Droigheann, Maighstir Rhyslin's First Bhanna. With me," she pointed to Ria, "is Ria, his second bhanna." The moment the words left her lips, the room seemed to brighten, light catching on leaves and paintings alike.

She wondered if she had overstepped her bounds when the woman paled and dropped to her knees.

"Please forgive me, Mistress," the young woman cried.

"I, we, didn't know."

Three other women appeared, drawn by the current of her voice, and upon hearing those words, they too knelt before Flur.

"We're sorry, Mistress, please don't tell Maighstir Rhyslin." The first woman groveled, bowing so low her forehead nearly touched the tiles. The tiles themselves seemed to thrum faintly with the pressure of her contrition.

"How may we serve you?" the second cried, holding her hands up to Flur and Ria, her voice trembling like a plucked string.

Flur tamped down her anger. "The— What did Maighstir Rhyslin call them — Automata?" When Ria nodded, Flur continued, "Will be here shortly with our luggage. When it arrives, you will take it to the rooms next to the Maighstir's chamber, and then you'll wait for us."

The third woman, one with cat's ears and a tail that flickered in distress, nodded. "Yes, Mistress, we will do as you say." Her tail lashed the air like a living metronome.

She leaned toward the golden-haired bhanna and sniffed, the motion quick, almost furtive. "You are looking for someone, yes?"

"Yes," Flur said after taking a minute to calm down. The tips of her ears tingled, the plants around her rustling faintly in sympathy.

She took a deep breath and slowly blew it out, the tension in the air easing with her exhale. "We are looking for Rowena. Can you show us where she is?"

The young woman's ears folded back when the seer was mentioned. "I can." Her tone made it evident that she didn't like Rowena.

"She's in the Maighstir's study." Flur watched attentively as her tail whipped from side to side, betraying more than her words did.

Ria took a few minutes to examine each woman's attire. All three wore maid dresses, one in blue, one in green, and the third in golden rod. The colors caught the lanternlight and shimmered faintly, as if the house itself claimed them.

As she saw the different shades, she wondered if Rhyslin had a house color but filed the thought for later and addressed the woman talking to Flur.

"We've given you our names. Would you give us yours?"

"I'm Mira," the third woman said, her ears pointed toward Ria. "She is Leena —" Mira gestured to the one in the blue dress, "and she's Ayla," she added, pointing at the one in green.

Flur's blue eyes sparkled as she watched the three maids. "I guess I can forgive you this time," she teased, extending a hand to Leena, who took it and rose to her feet.

Leena and Ayla sighed in relief, straightening their dresses as they watched Flur.

The room seemed to loosen its tension with them. "Thank you, Mistress. We'll wait here for your luggage and take it to your rooms. When you are finished with Rowena, Mira can show you to your room."

From her vantage, hiding under Ria's hair, the fairy silently laughed, rocking back and forth on the hin i-balanath's shoulder. The ripple of her amusement sent a faint shimmer through the strands, as if her mirth tugged at the light itself.

Flur nodded and turned to Mira. "Take us to Rowena, if you please.

Mira flashed a grin, her tail playfully dancing behind her as she led Flur, Ria, and the hidden Kita into the house and down the hallway.

Yet the air around her seemed charged, her golden-flecked eyes catching every flicker of light, her steps too sharp to mask the lash of irritation that twitched through her tail.

The two Hin I-Balanath followed her down a short hallway before turning right down another. Several times, Flur nudged Ria as she recognized paintings by artists she knew; each canvas seemed to glow briefly under her gaze, as if acknowledging her recognition. Ria, more reserved, offered only slight nods, but the air hummed faintly with her appreciation.

After turning left at the next intersection, they came to a tall oak door reinforced by three iron bands. The door radiated weight, a threshold that seemed to carry both memory and warning. Mira's ears perked forward as she indicated the barrier. "She's in there."

Her golden-flecked eyes fixed on Flur. "I'll wait out here for you." Her tail lashed angrily for a second or two before she mastered her temper, but the sharp gesture left the air tasting of ozone.

Flur smoothed out the wrinkles on her skirt, steadying her hands. "Ready?"

"Yes." The raven-haired bhanna nodded. "Let's get this over with. I hear that bathhouse calling me."

She gave a crooked grin, though her bond-thread hummed with unease. With confidence she didn't feel, Ria reached out and pushed the door open.

The door groaned as it swung, releasing a draft of cool air tinged with leather and ink. Directly before them stood a large oak desk with ornate carvings.

Atop it lay a leather-covered writing surface, inkwell, and feather quills that gleamed faintly, as though freshly dipped.

Behind the desk loomed a high-backed chair covered in black leather, and on the far wall, an ornamented Croabh gleamed with quiet power, much like the cabinets of the Dawn-Breaker.

Flur's breath caught; for a heartbeat she almost stepped back, the gravity of the place pressing against her resolve. Only Ria's nudge grounded her. She drew in a steadying breath and stepped forward, her skirts whispering against the intricately cut wooden planks, each line of the Croabh pattern seeming to guide her steps.

To the left, shelves sagged with neat ranks of leather-bound tomes, their spines whispering secrets too faint to hear.

Flur's fingers twitched with the ache to trace them, but Ria's small, knowing smile barred her.

To the right, a Darach-carved mantle
crowned the fireplace, its grain coiled like
captured flame.

A leather settee and a simple tree-trunk
chair stood sentinel beside it. The floors,
warm with polish, carried a subtle resonance,
as if they remembered countless footsteps
and waited to judge these new ones. Beyond,
double windows gazed out over the gardens,
where branches stirred though no wind
touched them.

At last, Flur's eyes found the young
woman seated in the plain chair. She looked
no older than four-and-twenty, long black
hair framing pale skin — not the pallor of
sickness but of a life confined indoors.

When her brown eyes lifted, shadows
clung to them, haunted, as though something
unseen gnawed at her spirit.

"Welcome home, Mistress," the young woman said as she rose and approached the two Hin I-Balanath. She dropped to her knees, the sound of it echoing in the chamber like a small plea. "My name is Rowena."

Ria's gaze swept over her, noting the conservatively cut black dress, its hem falling properly below the knees. Perfect. Too perfect. Rhyslin's type in all the obvious ways, quiet, pretty, compliant. Yet beneath the neatness, something unsettled her. She felt the press of a presence, heavy and veiled, and the thought came unbidden: *how much of this is Rowena, and how much is Despoina?*

There was only one way to know. "Before we start, can we speak with the Lady of Mystery, the all-seeing Despoina?"

Rowena gasped, her head snapping up toward Flur, who had moved behind the desk as though by instinct. "You can. When?"

"There is no time like the present," Ria said as she eased onto the settee. She crossed her legs, but tension whispered through her posture. "How may we do this?"

The seeress gestured toward a full-length mirror in the corner. "You'll be able to see her through the mirror."

Both of the hin I-Balanath turned toward it. The surface darkened, then coiled with smoke. A tall, willowy woman stepped forth in reflection — hair like obsidian smoke, body wrapped in a white gown from throat to ankle, its center pierced by a diamond gap girdled in leather spiral. An inverted crescent headdress gleamed with opals and emeralds. Her eyes were black pools scattered with silver flecks, stars drifting in the void. The smoke rolled outward, heavy with myrrh and ash, clinging to the chamber until even the books seemed to hold their breath.

"What do you wish, Flur Droigheann, former princess of Clann na Coille, now Bhanna to Mac Draoidheacd?"

"If it is not too inconvenient, we need to speak with Rowena and Rowena alone."

Flur's voice was steady, though her knees yearned to bend, her bond pulling taut at the weight of the goddess' presence.

The goddess turned, her gaze sliding to Ria. "Do you wish this as well, Ilyriatri, former Queen of Clann a' Fhasach?"

Ria bowed her head, her voice a chord of respect and steel. "I do, Milady of Mysteries. If Rowena wants to be Maighstir Rhyslin's bond, we need to know the real Rowena, not the Rowena receiving your help."

Despoina breathed deeply of the smoke, as if drawing in strands of future yet unwritten.

"Very well. I will not assist Rowena for the next two hours. She will have to muddle through your interview on her own."

The smoke recoiled into the mirror, leaving only Flur's reflection staring back, her blue eyes suddenly too mortal in the absence of the divine.

"Thank you," Flur murmured, offering a half-bow. She lowered herself into the leather chair behind the desk but shifted forward quickly, rejecting its comfort, leaning instead against the edge, a posture of judgment, not repose.

Rowena lifted her face from the floor. Without the goddess' aura upon her, she seemed smaller, her haunted eyes more fragile, her voice pleading: "Please don't throw me out."

When Flur gestured toward the plain wooden chair, Rowena recoiled as if it were a trap.

Slowly, hesitantly, she rose and sat, her every motion wary, like a bird fearing the snare.

Flur gave her an encouraging nod. "Now that it's just us, we—" she gestured to Ria, "have some questions. If we don't like what you say, throwing you out could be the least of our actions."

Rowena's lips trembled, her eyes brimming, but she forced them still. The floor beneath her chair thrummed faintly with her effort at composure. "I understand, Mistress."

From the moment Flur fixed her gaze on the raven-haired woman, the air seemed to tighten in the study. Shadows lengthened along the carved Croabh floor as if the wood itself were listening.

"Good." Flur eyed the woman, considering how to phrase her first question.

"How long have you been seeing things that eventually come true?"

It was apparent the seeress hadn't expected that question, for she grew even paler, if possible, and shivered. The lamplight flickered, dimming. "I've seen visions since I was five summers old."

Flur almost felt sorry for the young woman. To carry sight since childhood was no gift, but a burden of smoke and silence. She framed her next question, but Ria spoke first.

"Did they always come true?"

"No, not at first," Rowena answered quietly. Her voice carried like a ripple across still water.

Flur leaned forward slightly, catching that thread. "What did your parents think?"

The young woman's eyes dropped to the floor, her voice sinking with them.

"At first, they thought I was making things up, but after a few things came true, they started getting worried."

"About you or for themselves?" Ria asked, her tone even, but the hearth crackled as if in protest.

The seeress's quiet breath was the only sound for a long moment. "At first, I believe they were worried about me, but eventually, for themselves." She dared to look up at the two Hin I-Balanath with hope in her eyes, fragile as moth wings. "I think they feared that if too many things came true, they'd be blamed for harboring a daemon."

Flur locked eyes with Ria. The silence between them was heavy, like the moment before a bond-oath.

Then Flur asked the question neither wanted spoken. "What did your parents do as more and more of your predictions came true?"

"Momma tried to get the village priest to get rid of what she considered an evil spirit," Rowena said flatly, her voice devoid of tone. The windowpanes rattled, catching a ghost of old memory. "When the priest said there was no evil spirit, Daddy called him a fool, yanked me out of the church, and took me back home."

She shuddered, rocking slightly, as if the Croabh floor itself rocked with her. "He said he would beat the evil out of me." Her body swayed, a rhythm of old survival. "He beat me at every chance; if he didn't, then Momma would do it." Tears traced silver lines down her pale cheeks as she lifted her gaze toward Flur.

Flur's heart clenched, the edges of her bond with Rhyslin tugging hot with anger. For a breath, she saw him standing in judgment over Rowena's parents, saw the reckoning that might have been. She swallowed it down.

"How long did the beating go on?" Her own voice cracked like brittle glass.

"For five years, right up until Mistress Despoina sent one of her disciples to take me to her temple." Rowena raised her hands to Flur, almost pleading, as if seeking absolution she could not name.

Ria's hand moved gently to her shoulder, grounding her. "How long were you at the Temple?"

Rowena's pain softened into warmth. "I stayed with the Oracles for eight years." She closed her eyes, then opened them again, brighter for a heartbeat. "I left when I turned eighteen and ended up here. Maighstir Rhyslin let me stay, asking for very little."

Flur's brow furrowed as memory tugged at her. "Mathair mentioned something that Astinmah said about Maighstir Darkblade knowing about the Orcan attack."

She fixed Rowena with a sharper look. "Was that your doing?"

"I saw the attack in a dream and told Maighstir Rhyslin about it. He chose to act on it." Her voice was wistful, the fire lowering to embers as though it grieved with her.

Ria tilted her head, catching the sadness. "Did you also see the chance we would bond with him?"

When Rowena nodded, the raven-haired hin i-balanath matron sighed, heavy as wind through barren branches. "You could have kept that to yourself, and we would have never come here."

The seeress bit her lip until it whitened. "I couldn't have lived with myself if your people had ended up as slaves." Tears welled again, shimmering in the firelight. "Even if it meant that he would bond with you—"

she gazed at Flur, "or you, " her eyes shifted to Ria, "and that I would be thrown away like an old blanket."

Flur leaned against the desk, her fingers caressing the leather writing surface as if to ground herself. "You made a hard decision, and we thank you for it." She tucked a loose strand of hair behind her ear, though her ears flushed pink.

"Why do you want to stay, and why did you ask him five times to bond with you?"

When the raven-haired seeress answered, her voice was so fragile that both Hin I-Balanath leaned closer to catch it. "Because I think I love him."

Ria gave a slow nod, her eyes softening. "You don't know for sure, do you?"

Rowena shook her head, shame lowering her lashes. "I was always afraid to ask, for he's never paid me much mind or said anything about how he feels."

71

Flur's brow arched. "The Lady of Mysteries has never hinted at how he feels?"

Another shake of Rowena's head. "She's kept very silent about it. I've suspected that she can't read his future."

The room stilled at that, as though the Croabh floor itself hushed.

Flur gave her next question lightly, like tossing a stone into still water. "Why wait here for Maighstir Rhyslin?"

Rowena looked embarrassed, folding her hands. "He won't allow me in his study if he's not there."

Flur chuckled softly and caught Ria's attention. [Doesn't that sound like him?]

Ria's lips curved faintly. [It does.]

Flur's thought brushed like warmth across the bond-thread. [I'd feel sad if we said no. She seems truthful.]

Ria tilted her head slightly left, her agreement blooming like a sigh through the air. [She does, and she's not lying about loving him. Shall we?]

When Flur nodded, the unspoken consent hung in the room like incense.

Ria pulled Rowena into a soft embrace, and the seeress clung as though she'd been drowning all her life and had at last found air. The Croabh patterns in the floor glowed faintly, as if witnessing a new chord struck in Rhyslin's household.

"Let's get you ready to bond with your Maighstir."

Chapter Four

Where Water and Love Are Woven

Rana had only needed a few breaths to slip into a light sleep, her head pillowed against Rhyslin's shoulder. The draoidh stilled, remembering how Ria had once leaned on him in the same trust. He closed his eyes, letting his breath fall into the cadence of meditation. Around them, the grove hushed, cicadas softening their song, leaves above whispering in a rhythm that matched his own heart.

A shadow stirred against his senses. He cracked an eye, expecting perhaps a cloud crossing the sun, but found instead that the willow's branches had bent low, their green fingers spreading wide to cast a deeper shade upon him.

The scent of resin and damp earth thickened, like the tree itself exhaled.

Tilting his head back, he caught sight of her, the fox-eared dryad, perched along a wide branch. Her amber eyes gleamed with mischief as she mouthed a word down to him: *Mac Draoidheachd.* The willow's voice made flesh, acknowledging his place.

When he arched a brow, she flashed him a grin and sprawled upon the branch, her tail dangling, swaying in a slow, lazy arc. Every few heartbeats, it stirred the air, fanning the scent of crushed willow leaves. When Rana roused a short time later, the draoidh noted the tail's quickened tempo, a silent herald of waking hearts.

The young spell-blade hummed as she stretched, the motion carrying a feline languor.

Hazel eyes blinked open, widened, and her lips parted in a soft *O* at the sight of the dryad.

Without tearing her gaze away, she tapped Rhyslin's thigh, her pulse racing loud enough that even the branches seemed to quiver with her.

Rhyslin tapped back, amused, as the dryad lifted a paw in greeting, tail swishing in playful rhythm.

"She's awake," Rana whispered, voice full of wonder.

"I see that," Rhyslin murmured, raising his hand in a gesture half-greeting, half-blessing. "Good afternoon, *Nighean na craoibhe*."

The willow's leaves shivered as though in answer.

"Good day, *Mac Draoidheachd*," the dryad purred, paw pressing flat against the branch as if to steady herself within her home.

"This one is known as Cansasa. This one wants to thank you for not hurting her home."

"If I did, Matron Fohgar would bury me alive," he replied with mock severity, though the staff at his side hummed faintly in agreement.

Cansasa's laughter rippled down like shaken leaves. "Cansasa understands. This one has been asleep a long time." Her amber gaze flicked to Rana, who squirmed, drawing the spirit's attention like a moth to flame. "What is it, young one?"

"Maighstir Rhyslin said you had been asleep as long as he'd been here. What woke you up?" Rana asked, curiosity softening her voice.

The dryad pointed, paw delicate as a blessing. "Love woke me. This one could feel the love you have for each other."

The air itself thickened, warm with the fragrance of blossoms stirred out of season. Rana blushed, and the willow seemed to lean closer, its branches bowing like listening ears.

"Are the two of you not lovers?" Cansasa asked bluntly.

Rhyslin hesitated. Even the cicadas paused. "We are still working out exactly what our relationship is," he said carefully. "Her mother and I are bonded."

The dryad tilted forward, amber gaze sharp as foxfire. "But this one felt her love for you, and your love for her."

Rana's blush deepened, her breath hitching. She pressed closer, her words spilling with the tremor of long-held truth.

"If I could, I would bond with Maighstir Rhyslin. I've been seeing him in my dreams for eight years. He's the first man to pay attention to me and take me as I am."

The willow trembled from root to crown, releasing a sigh of leaves. Cansasa's right ear perked, tail sweeping faster. "It makes sense. From such things, affections grow." Her eyes slid toward the draoidh. "What about you, Mac Draoidheachd?"

"How can I not love her?" he answered, voice low and cryptic, but the ground beneath them thrummed in approval. "She is part of my new family." With that, he braced his staff, rising with a fluid motion. "It was a pleasure to meet you, Cansasa." He offered a half-bow. The willow bent its limbs in mirror, as though bowing with her.

"I promised to show Rana the bathhouse," he added.

Cansasa's grin widened, fox-tail swaying. "This one does sense all the water, Mac Draoidheachd." She waved her paw toward Rana. "This one thinks you will enjoy it, little one."

With a languid stretch, she melded into bark and vanished into her tree, leaving behind a faint musk of sap and rainwater.

"How does she know where the water is?" Rana whispered, wonder still in her eyes. "How does she know that I'll enjoy it?" She brushed her skirt smooth with trembling hands, then stood, slipping instinctively to Rhyslin's right side.

"Dryads can sense water," Rhyslin explained, tone gentle for her sake. "Through their roots, they can localize springs or wells within ten feet."

Rana nodded, her hazel eyes bright as riverlight. She reached for his hand and clasped it firmly, her smile quiet but sure. "You promised to amaze me with your bathhouse."

The willow behind them rustled one last time, as though sealing a covenant.

The draoidh chuckled, the sound low and warm as water over stone, and stepped out from under the willow's shelter. "Prepare to be amazed," he teased, his staff tapping softly against the path as he guided her toward the manor.

The air shifted as they rounded the corner, cool shade giving way to a hushed reverence. A side entrance opened before them, framed by ivy and two statues of Mathair Astinmah: one serene in sleep, the other caught mid-step, as if about to enter flowing waters. Their marble eyes glimmered faintly in the afternoon light, and Rana felt them watching.

Inside, the air was heavier, thick with the mineral tang of water. She drew a breath and tasted it on her tongue, ancient, cleansing, alive. The vestibule pressed in like a hushed chapel, stone walls whispering the echo of unseen streams.

Rhyslin's touch at her shoulder recalled her from reverie; she blinked as he gestured to an open doorway.

"You can change in that room and come back out here. I'll be waiting."

"Okay." She released his hand reluctantly, stepping into the chamber. It smelled faintly of lavender oil and damp linen, and her footfalls were softened by smooth-tiled floors. Along one wall stood cubicles for clothing, and benches waited like patient attendants.

She hummed softly as she slid her blouse from her shoulders, folding it carefully before placing it away. The rustle of fabric seemed louder in the sanctity of the room.

"What do I change into?" she called, fingers loosening the ties of her skirt. The fabric pooled around her ankles like fallen petals.

From his own chamber, Rhyslin's voice carried, calm and grounding. "There should be a yakuta hanging on the wall. Once you are out here, we'll wash the dust off and get into the pools."

Her hazel eyes found the garment at last: a wrap of pale cloth, its weave faintly shimmering in the lamplight. She held it to her chest, cheeks flushing at its brevity, the hem brushing barely mid-thigh.

Did he mean for her to wear this into the pool? The thought warmed her skin with a guilty thrill. She tied it about herself, the linen whispering against her body, and peeked around the corner.

There he stood, waiting. A towel slung low about his waist, his presence filled the chamber like a pillar of calm strength.

"Is this, okay?" she asked, twirling, the yakuta flaring softly.

"You look fine." His smile was steady as
he slipped an arm around her shoulders.
"Are you ready?"

She leaned into him, her heart steadied
by his nearness. Together they stepped into
the frigidarium, and Rana's breath caught.
The chamber opened wide, its vaulted ceiling
painted with celestial constellations, its air
sharp with the bite of cold stone.

A vast pool stretched before them, so
deep and clear it mirrored the frescoes above
in a trembling reflection.

"How deep is it?" she whispered, awed.

Without hesitation, the draoidh shed his
towel and stepped into the water. Ripples
flared outward, striking the tiles like silver
rings. "At the deepest, it comes to my
shoulders," he said, moving into the
shadowed depths.

The young spell-blade hesitated at the edge. The water smelled of stone and ice, its surface reflecting her flushed cheeks. She dipped a toe and shivered, the cold biting up her spine. For a long moment, she warred with herself. Then, drawing a steadying breath, she stepped forward, choosing courage over fear.

The water closed around her legs, her body stiffening at each new depth. She paused as it kissed her hidden flower, again as it lapped over her breasts. Then, gathering resolve, she untied the yakuta and let it fall beside his towel. Her head rose high, proud despite the blush that painted her skin, as she walked deliberately down the slope.

Submerging, she leaned back until the icy water crowned her head. Rising again, she tossed her hair free, strands streaming down her back like molten glass.

The pool itself seemed to shiver with her bravery, the painted stars overhead glimmering faintly as if approving.

Rhyslin's eyes softened, his voice a low murmur of claim and invitation. "Come here, mo phrìseil."

"Seadh, mhaighstir," Rana whispered, half-floating as she threw herself into his arms. He caught her with effortless strength, anchoring her against his side. Her cheek rested against the steady drum of his heart. "Is this it?"

The draoidh shook his head, lips brushing her temple. "No, this is just the first room. We still have an amar blàth and an linne teth to go through."

Her voice was hushed as prayer. "When do we take those steps?"

"When you are ready. We won't do anything that you are uncomfortable with."

She closed her eyes, letting the rhythm of his heartbeat and the cold's sharpness give way to warmth inside.

Slowly, she loosened, the water no longer feeling hostile but cleansing. After a long silence, she whispered, "I think I'm ready to go to the next pool."

Without a word, Rhyslin pulled himself out of the frigidarium, steam rolling from his skin like a second cloak, and extended a hand to Rana. When she nodded, he gave a sharp tug that lifted her free of the water as if she weighed nothing, setting her gently on the tiles beside him.

The chill clung to her body like a jealous lover. Gooseflesh marbled her arms, and beads of water traced cold paths down her spine. She wondered, breath catching, why it felt *colder out here than in the pool itself.*

The silence pressed in like stone, and when she began to shiver, Rhyslin drew her against him.

His arm felt like a band of living heat, guiding her toward the arch that opened into the next chamber.

Crossing the threshold into the tepidarium was like passing from a cavern's shadow into a meadow at springtide. The very air shifted, soft, fragrant, touched with herbs and faint floral oils that whispered of Astinmah's breath. Each droplet that slid down her back seemed to dissolve into warmth, no longer stabbing her skin but caressing it.

Rana halted, stretching instinctively, caught by the frescoes. "Oh, how beautiful," she murmured, voice hushed as if before an altar.

The nearest wall shimmered with paint depicting A' Mhathair Astinmah strolling unclad through fields of wildflowers, petals seeming to bend toward her in eternal devotion.

Rhyslin let her wander, her pale feet tapping lightly across the tiles, while he sank into the pool. Leaning back against the curved lip of stone, he studied her.

She bent over a mosaic, dark hair tumbling like a cascade of ink, and in that moment he thought she looked less like a girl than a dryad freed from bark, caught mid-dance among painted blossoms. The thought lingered so deeply that he scarcely noticed when her gaze flicked to him, catching the weight of his eyes.

Feeling daring, Rana gave in to the wicked impulse curling through her chest.

Pretending not to see him, she gathered her hair and let it spill in a waterfall down her shoulders, then lifted her arms into a languid stretch that arched every line of her body.

For a heartbeat, the frescoes themselves seemed to brighten, blossoms along the wall glowing faintly in sympathy with her display.

Rhyslin was not fooled. He narrowed his eyes, lifted his hand, and beckoned. The gesture was subtle, but the room seemed to lean with it, waiting.

For a moment she froze, caught between terror and exhilaration. Then, with deliberate care, she stepped toward him.

The arch of her ankle, the roll of her hips, each movement became a rhythm, and with every step the air thickened with something older than either of them. By the time she padded across the edge of the pool, the bounce of her body carried like music, rippling across the water.

Rhyslin's breath caught, she stalked toward him like a wild feline tamed by choice alone.

He marveled at how far she had come in mere weeks. She dipped a toe into the pool, sending concentric ripples out that shimmered like light through glass. Finding it warm, she slipped inside and drifted to his side, curling into him as naturally as if the water had delivered her there.

"This is much better, maighstir. I could sit here like this all day." She nuzzled into his shoulder, sigh soft as a prayer. "I never thought I could be comfortable." Her lips quirked in a mischievous smile. "If I were older, would you bond with me?" she teased.

Rhyslin rested his head against hers, breath warm at her ear. "I can, if you wish — but it can change your destiny."

His whisper drew a flush to the tip of her ear, darkening its brown shade.

Rana shivered. She wanted what he offered yet feared it too. She wanted to be loved but trembled before the weight of fate. And in that moment, for the first time in eight years, she realized the murmurs that haunted her had fallen silent. The air itself seemed to hush in reverence.

Rather than answer, she pressed closer, snuggling against him until not even the water could slip between them. And in the stillness, with silence in her ears and warmth in her heart, she promised herself that one day she would ask him to bond with her.

Chapter Five
The Gift in the Tepidarium

The thick oak door loomed before them, its grain darkened by centuries of steam and whispered vows. The air itself seemed hushed, as though the manor knew what step was about to be taken. A faint breath of warmth curled beneath the threshold, carrying the mineral tang of stone and water.

"Where would have they entered from?" Ria inquired, her palm brushing reverently across the old wood. Through the bond, Flur caught the faint thrum of her anticipation, a heartbeat echo beneath her own.

Rowena lifted one pale hand and threaded it through her raven hair, her fingers trembling just enough for the other two to notice.

"If you left them near that old willow tree, they'll come up and enter from the west doorway."

She gestured vaguely, though her eyes never left the heavy door before them. "They'll enter through a door like this, change in the changing rooms, and soak in the frigidarium before going to the tepidarium."

Her grin was crooked, almost self-deprecating, as though speaking of warmth could shield her from the cold of doubt rising inside her.

"Are there any more entrances?" Flur asked eagerly, nearly bouncing on her heels.

Excitement flickered through the bond she shared with Ria, bright and crackling, like sparks leaping from kindling.

"Of course, there are," Rowena replied, the words spilling out in a rush, as though relieved to be useful.

"This door leads to one of the changing rooms between the frigidarium and the tepidarium." She glanced at Flur's wide eyes, softened by her own nervous smile. "I've never liked the cold bath and have always entered here."

Her grin faltered as she caught the younger woman's look of suspicion. "No, I've never shared the bath with him. He wouldn't let me."

The air shifted. A single bead of condensation traced down the oak, catching light like a tear.

"How did you know what she was going to ask?" Ria's voice was low, though the bond carried her doubt clearly.

Rowena chuckled, though she worried at her lip immediately after. "Did Lady Despoina help me? No, she didn't."

She seemed amused when both women blinked, as if expecting the goddess's hand in all things. "I don't have to be a seeress to understand how people think," she explained. "I just have to pay attention."

She twisted a lock of her hair around one finger until the knuckle whitened, her eyes lowering. "Maighstir Rhyslin never wanted to be alone with any of the women here. Not me, nor any of the servants." The words dropped heavily, and for a moment even the wood beneath their hands seemed to darken, drawing the weight of her confession into its grain.

"It's almost as if he were worried about what might happen." A breath caught in her throat. "Is he really going to accept me?"

Ria reached forward and gently unwound the tangled strand from Rowena's finger, as though breaking a spell.

The bond shimmered warm between them, carrying reassurance like a steadying hand. "Yes. Once we speak to him, you will become his treas bhanna." She smiled softly, and the tremor in Rowena's shoulders eased as hope lit her eyes.

"I hope you're ready for the bonding," Ria added, the oak door groaning faintly in the silence that followed. "I can promise you it's like nothing you've ever felt."

Flur nodded, her golden hair catching the faint glow of lamplight, her excitement rolling through the bond like sunlight spilling over frost.

"I felt like I was drifting in the clouds and wrapped in Cotan when he bonded me." She blushed deeply, surprising Rowena, then admitted, "I lost myself in the bond for the first three days."

Ria scoffed lightly, brushing Flur's shoulder. "Just the first three days? You still get lost in the bond."

Rowena's eyes widened at the playful admission, and Flur gave a helpless little shrug. "She's right. But then, so does she. All Ria wants to do is cuddle."

"I won't deny it." Ria lifted her chin, her voice touched with mock indignity, but the warmth in the bond belied her tone. "I feel safe in his arms," she admitted, her gaze softening. "It will be different for you, but only if it's you and not Despoina."

For an instant, the faintest smile ghosted across her lips, as though the goddess's presence brushed against them all. "The fact that he cares for my daughter only makes it better."

The corridor seemed to draw a deeper breath of its own as Rowena's gaze went glassy.

A shiver of unseen current stirred her raven hair, though no draft touched the others.

"Your daughter," her voice rang hollow, layered as if two tones spoke at once, one human, one eternal. Her chin lifted, eyes unfocused and terrible. **"Is she here?"**

The air thickened; a low hum trembled through the oak door at their backs, as if the wood itself recognized who spoke.

Ria's lips parted, her breath catching. She knew that cadence, that weight pressing against her chest like the first judgment of a tribunal. "Lady Despoina," she whispered, blinking against the sudden sting in her eyes. Her voice cracked.

"Yes, she's here and with Maighstir Rhyslin." The goddess's gaze pinned her, and she faltered, stammering like a child. "I—I don't know if he's changed her destiny."

She closed her eyes, her heart pounding in prayer. "Has he changed her future?"

Rowena's arm rose, stiff and unnatural, her hand tilting as though she cradled scales only she could see. The air around her seemed to ripple like heated glass.

"It is murky, even for me to see," the goddess admitted, her words resonant, trembling the very stone beneath their feet. **"But I do not believe he's changed the future."**

Ria sagged forward, a strangled sound escaping her throat. **"Thank A' Mathair."** She pressed her palm to her chest as though steadying her own heart. Her voice turned fragile, desperate, the plea of a mother before the divine. "Would it be possible for him to train her so she can better survive what's to come?"

The silence that followed stretched taut, full of the goddess's unspoken weight. Even Flur, still and wide-eyed, felt the ache of it inside her bond, like a pressure along her bones.

At last, Rowena's lifted hand shifted again, as though her unseen scales tipped beneath new knowledge. **"I do not know. But from what I can determine, it could increase her odds."**

She tilted her head as if listening, though no one else could hear. A shadow crossed her expression, then softened. Her voice, though still otherworldly, carried a strange gentleness. **"Very well, my dear Rowena. I'll leave you alone now to experience your bonding."**

The glaze broke. Rowena's body shuddered, her knees buckling slightly as she drew in ragged gulps of air, panting like a swimmer dragged back from drowning.

The humming silence collapsed, leaving only the sound of their own breaths in the corridor.

The oak door gave a low groan as Ria pressed it open, warm breath of mineral-scented steam rolling out to meet them. The air clung heavy, tinged with lavender oil from the tepidarium beyond. Stone tiles whispered with condensation under their feet, slick with the passage of countless bathers.

"Come along, Flur," Ria said, her arm steady around the trembling seeress. "We have a gift to prepare for our beloved Maighstir."

Rowena's steps faltered as they crossed the threshold, the ancient hinges sighing shut behind them like a seal on her fate.

"Strip," Ria commanded. Her voice carried like a bell in the mist, low and unyielding.

Rowena froze, the warmth of the room washing over her even as a shiver climbed her back. A strange blush bloomed beneath her skin, spreading like sunrise from her collarbone down her chest. Droplets condensed along the curve of her neck, tracing her pulse as if the chamber itself marked her hesitation.

"If you can't be naked with us," Ria added, pointing toward the far door, "you can't do it with him."

"Yes, Mistress," Rowena whispered, the words trembling into the steam. With trembling fingers, she loosened the buttons of her blouse. The garment fell soundlessly to the wet stone, followed by her skirt. The chamber seemed to hold its breath as the soft blush deepened, her body revealed in the perfumed haze.

Flur inhaled sharply, her breath fogging the air. She was surprised by the seeress's beauty, curves made luminous by steam-slick light. Rowena's hips swayed slightly as she shifted, her breasts full, her skin beaded with dew like a flower after rainfall. The sight stirred a primal recognition in Flur — if they were in the courts of Bazan, Rowena would be paraded as a *traill-feise*, clothed in silk and chains, desired and displayed. The thought quickened Flur's breath.

Ria mirrored her astonishment. "Oh my," she uttered softly, voice carrying reverence. "She'd give Rana a run for her money." The older woman rummaged among the cubicles, the sound of wooden doors creaking, until she pulled free three Yakuta robes.

"I can't decide whether to let her wear this — or make her go out there as she is."

"I know." Flur circled Rowena like a flame licking dry tinder. "It would be like a Yuletide gift for him to unwrap. We could make her go to him wearing just a leash."

The word echoed in the chamber. The seeress's breath caught as the image seared into her mind: crawling to Rhyslin on hands and knees, steam curling along her back, the leash taut between her wrists. Heat rushed through her so suddenly she thought the bath had reached her skin already.

"She likes the thought of that," Ria murmured knowingly as Rowena shivered. "Don't you, caileag thràilleil?"

"Yes, Mistress, I do," Rowena admitted, voice barely audible over the steady drip of water into the distant pools. Her confession seemed to thrum in the stone walls, as if the bathhouse itself absorbed her surrender.

105

A devious grin curved Flur's lips. "How about the best of both? Wrap her in one of these, then let him order her to strip. He'll appreciate the leash."

"You heard the ciad cheangail, caileag thràilleil. Put this on," Ria said firmly, handing her a Yakuta. "Make yourself look good for your Maighstir."

"Yes, Mistress," Rowena murmured. The robe's linen clung damply to her skin as she slipped it on, her fingers tying the bow in a trembling knot. She smoothed the fabric down, gasping when she realized how scandalously short it was. The hem stopped mid-thigh; if she bent even slightly, the robe would bare her fully. The thought struck her with equal measures of dread and desire. "I don't know if I can do this," she whispered, eyes wide as a child's, looking to Flur.

"Are you sure?" Flur asked, her brow arching. When Rowena nodded, the golden-haired bhanna smirked. "That's too bad. You'll have to wait to be bonded. Ria and I can keep him busy for several months. He won't have time to think of you." Her laughter rippled like a brook. "And if Rana is doing what I think she's doing, she'll be the next bond."

Her teasing was punctuated by the sound of silk whispering as Flur stripped down, slipping into her own Yakuta. She tied it to accentuate her breasts, tugging the hem higher so her thighs gleamed in the steam. "So, what will it be?"

Rowena lifted her hands, crossing her wrists in silent plea. Her offering was met with Flur's deft fingers, the leash tied snug around them.

Flur gave it a tug, the sound of leather sliding through her hand sharp in the mist.

"Come along, caileag thràilleil. Maighstir Rhyslin's waiting."

"Wait for me," Ria called, hastily wrapping herself in her robe, leaving it provocatively loose. "I can't wait to see his expression when we present her."

Cloth rustled as they gathered the discarded garments into the cubicles. Then Flur pulled the leash again, playful, insistent. "Let's go, tràill-feise."

Rowena followed, heart hammering as the heat of the tepidarium wrapped around her. They entered the space between frigidarium and warmth, steam curling like veils around their bodies. Across the pool, two discarded robes lay abandoned.

"She got brave," Flur murmured with a smirk. "It's about time."

"Shush," Ria scolded. "I still think she's too young."

"She's just eighteen," Flur countered with a wicked giggle, tugging the leash again. "This one is about the same age, give or take a few years."

Rowena blushed hotly, daring at last to lift her eyes. Across the haze of the tepidarium, she saw him, Rhyslin, his dark form half-reclined, and the young woman nestled against him. Jealousy sparked like flint in her chest. The Hin I-Balanath in his arms was radiant, beautiful, a rival already basking in the comfort Rowena longed for.

Her body ached to break away, to crawl across the tiles and lay her bond at his feet. But fear kept her tethered to Flur's hand. Fear of rejection. Fear of being cast out.

When Ria growled and turned back to fetch fresh robes, Rowena drew a shaky breath. Her leash slackened for the first time.

For a heartbeat, she considered bolting forward. But then she remembered, Flur's teasing could become exile if she disobeyed.

So she stayed, trembling, heat licking at her thighs, steam curling around her like the goddess's gaze. Waiting to be led, waiting to be seen.

Without saying a word, Flur tugged on the leash. The motion was sharp enough to pull Rowena forward, her bare feet slipping against the damp tiles.

Steam curled thickly around them, carrying the mineral tang of the tepidarium, and her breath quickened as the sure-footed bhanna half-dragged her toward the glow of the warm pool.

"Maighstir Rhyslin, Ria, and I have brought you a gift." Flur's chirpy tone rang bright, almost jarring against the hush of the chamber.

The sound grated on Rowena's nerves, and for an instant she longed to shove the golden-haired caid-cheangail into the pool. Instead, she inhaled the wet heat and reminded herself to be patient.

The surface of the frigidarium shimmered faintly in her peripheral vision, but all her attention snapped forward at the sound of a soft voice.

The young woman nestled against Rhyslin's side stirred, her eyelids heavy with drowsy pride. "Momma, I did it. I crossed through the Linne fuar."

The goddess's breath seemed to linger on the water itself. Ria's expression softened as she gazed at her daughter. Then, when her eyes lifted to meet Rhyslin's, her robe slid from her shoulders like falling petals. She set it neatly beside the other two, then stepped into the pool, the water parting with a soft, reverent sigh as if recognizing her presence.

111

She crossed to his side and curled into the curve of his arm, where he welcomed her as if she had always belonged there.

"What did I tell you? She's a cuddlebug," Flur whispered, her breath brushing Rowena's ear. She poked the seeress, breaking the trance of her gaze. "I can't blame her."

The golden-haired bhanna's deft fingers worked quickly, the leash unknotted, Rowena's borrowed garment slipping away like mist until the leather draped around her neck in quiet claim. The sound of it brushing her skin made her shiver. Flur joined the others, shedding her own garment, sinking into the steaming water with a ripple that caught the torchlight. She propelled herself forward, rising from the pool before Rhyslin, water beading across her lifted breasts as she leaned in and kissed him hungrily.

"We find her acceptable, Maighstir. You may bond her." Her voice, breathless and damp with desire, drifted like incense over the warm water.

The draoidh's hazel eyes sparked as though catching the reflection of the braziers.

He reached and tapped Flur lightly on the cheek. "Oh? As if I need your permission to bond another woman."

The weight of his tone settled over them like thunder before a storm. Even the water stilled, as if listening.

Flur blinked in shock, then lowered her head quickly. "Yes, Maighstir."

Rhyslin's fingers cupped her chin, tilting her face until her eyes met his. "Flur Dris, my Ciad-Cheangail, Keeper of my hearts, you and Ria were granted *deas-ghnàth a' chiad diùltadh*. While it would have made your thoughts known, it is not a blanket by which to tell me what I may and may not do."

His words were calm, but the bond thrummed with his displeasure. Both Flur and Ria felt the reverberation, like distant chimes struck within their chests.

When Flur hurriedly nodded, subdued, Rhyslin's gaze swept to Ria, who remained steady, implacable, as if carved from the stone walls themselves. To his left, Rana's eyes glimmered with curiosity, the girl silent, watchful, storing every gesture and word. With a sigh, the draoidh turned his gaze fully upon Rowena.

"Rowena, do you wish to offer your bond?"

The seeress nearly forgot to breathe. His gaze bore into her, stripping her of every pretense. For a heartbeat she felt the weight of every destiny she had glimpsed as a seeress, and yet none had terrified her as much as this moment.

She wanted him to command her, to strip the choice away. But he only waited.

Her lungs burned, and she forced a breath. "Yes, Maighstir, I do."

The faintest smile touched his lips, as though he had always known. "Then come and perform the ritual."

Her knees trembled as she stepped carefully into the pool. Warm water lapped against her thighs as she knelt, finding a place where she could bow her head and still keep it above the surface. Her voice, quivering yet resolute, filled the chamber like a prayer.

"I, Rowena Auldsotir, offer my bond, asking for nothing in return. In Ananke's name do I ask this."

The name of the Oathbinder seemed to thrum through the bathhouse itself. Torches guttered, steam thickened, and the water hushed. She held her breath, heart pounding as she prayed he would accept her.

When she opened her eyes, his hazel gaze was waiting. She fell into them as though into a vast sky, laid bare before him in body and soul.

"I accept your bond," he intoned, each word carrying the weight of law and god-fire. "And promise to treat you the way you need to be treated. I will love you, protect you, and make you part of my house. This I swear by Ananke, the Oathbinder."

The bond settled over her like a mantle of light and warmth. For an instant she swore she felt invisible threads binding her to him, weaving her spirit into his. A sob burst free, and she flew into his arms, clinging to him as tears spilled freely.

"Thank you, thank you, thank you," she whispered against his skin.

Rana made a small, startled sound, blinking herself awake just in time to see him cradle Rowena close.

Steam curled around them like a benediction, and Rana silently vowed that one day she would feel the same embrace.

Rhyslin tilted Rowena's tear-streaked face upward. "Why were you afraid?"

"That you would throw me out," she admitted, voice small as a child's.

His lips brushed her temple as he whispered, "It was never going to happen."

The water itself seemed to sigh with relief, and the torches steadied, their flames burning brighter as if to mark the household's new bond.

Chapter Six

Of Joy in the Morning and Oaths by Night

"That was delightful," the golden-haired bhanna murmured, the next morning, as she rolled over in bed, her arm draping across Rhyslin's chest.

With a low mumble of his own, the draoidh dipped his head to kiss her shoulder. "Was it everything you expected it to be?"

"Mmhmm." Flur burrowed into his right side, her breath warm against his skin. "I'm going to use that bathhouse every night. I've never been in anything so luxurious." She turned her head, gazing across his chest to where Ria still rested. "Is she awake yet?"

Rhyslin yawned, stretching, then reached down toward his second bhanna. "I dunno, let's find out," he whispered, crooking two fingers in preparation to tickle her ribs.

But the auburn-haired bhanna caught his wrist with practiced ease. "Don't think about it, Meleth nín," Ria mumbled, nestling closer against his left shoulder. She pressed a kiss to his chest. "I'm awake. What are our plans for today?"

Flur stilled, waiting, her bright eyes fixed on him.

Another yawn racked the draoidh. Outside the chamber, faint morning birdsong mingled with the hush of the household stirring. "It depends. If Meron wakes, I need to speak with him about the accusations Ixa and Andros made."

He paused, voice softening. "If he doesn't, then I'll talk with them about making their lives easier."

Ria stretched, her lips brushing his again before she pulled reluctantly away. "Oh? In what way?"

Rhyslin moaned faintly at her withdrawal, then gazed into her green eyes. "I need to see if they can work the ship without being bound to the crystal. If they can, I can hire more elementals for other vessels."

Flur lifted her head, her tone gentle. "Not to mention Ixa could live with Rembran and be happy. She deserves that — I think he's good for her." She leaned in, brushing her lips against his.

"You make a good point," Rhyslin murmured, gathering both women in his arms.

"I always do." Flur giggled, pushing upright to stretch, golden hair spilling in the morning light. "Speaking of always being right — when will you consummate your bond with Rowena?"

Rhyslin's eyes lingered on her as temptation stirred.

He debated reaching for her, then thought better of it. "Tonight, I think."

Ria poked his side, arching a dark brow. "Think? That's nebulous." Her mock glare held its own heat.

He raised his left hand in surrender. "Okay, okay. Tonight, for sure."

"Good." Ria kissed his cheek, smug as a queen. "Have I told you lately what a good man you are?"

"I think you mentioned it somewhere after your fourth rapture last night," he teased, drawing a groan of embarrassment from her.

"Yes, you're a good man," Flur echoed, gifting him another kiss. "Tha gaol agam ort, mo maighstir iongantach[1]," she whispered, her hand sliding down his body.

---

[1] I love you, my wonderful master

"Haven't you had enough, you tràill gnè?" Ria teased, catching her bond-sister's hand. "We can't spend all day in bed. We have things to do."

"Fine," Flur groused, stealing one last kiss before slipping away. "A shame. I was going to eat him alive."

"I'm spared from the dreadful task of satisfying the insatiable one," Rhyslin quipped, making her blush. "I'll meet you both at noon."

He crossed to the armoire, pulling free a pair of pants, a soft blue shirt, and house shoes. By the time he had dressed, the warmth of the sheets had faded, and Flur and Ria had already vanished down the hall, laughter trailing faintly in their wake.

As Rhyslin walked into the hallway, the polished oak floors creaked faintly beneath his steps.

Warm morning light streamed in from narrow windows, painting the air in gold. He smiled absently, wondering why he hadn't bonded long ago.

Having two bhanna was different than he had ever imagined, both more chaotic and more complete. He was so lost in thought he didn't hear the two young women stalking behind him.

Rana moved like a shadow, her bare feet whispering against the floorboards. The raven-haired seeress beside her tried to mimic the spell-blade's movements, but the faint shuffle of her nightgown betrayed her. Rowena cringed at the sound, but Rana's grin widened, she looked like a cat about to pounce on a bird.

Rhyslin nearly jumped out of his skin when both young women leapt onto him, wrapping their arms around his frame.

"Good morning, Maighstir," Rana chirped, standing on tiptoes to plant a kiss on his cheek.

"Yes, good morrow, Maighstir," Rowena echoed, her blush rising hot against her pale skin.

"For goddess' sake, you gave me a start," Rhyslin groused, though his arms closed around them with warmth. "How did you sleep last night?"

"Well, enough, once we ran out of things to talk about," Rana said, tossing her hair over her shoulder with careless grace.

Once, Rhyslin might have worried what two women whispered about in the night. But in the last three weeks, he had learned that their talk, however focused on him, was not to be feared. "What did you talk about?"

Rowena tried for nonchalance, but the faint color in her cheeks betrayed her. "Oh, you know, just things."

Rana giggled. "It's mostly about you, Aon Socair." Her hazel eyes sparkled. "Are you going to eat breakfast?"

Rhyslin nodded. "Would you like to join me?"

Both women assented quickly. Rowena leaned into his side for a moment, almost unconsciously. "Yes, please. We're famished."

"Then, by all means, let's go get something to eat," Rhyslin said, draping his right arm around Rowena and his left around Rana as they walked the corridor.

"Maighstir," Rana whispered, her lips brushing his ear, "I think Rowena is pulling my leg."

"About?" His eyebrow arched in quiet amusement.

"She said I could get anything I wanted to eat. Is she telling the truth?"

Her narrowed eyes and hopeful tone made her sound like a child probing the boundaries of indulgence.

"She's not pulling your leg," Rhyslin admitted. "You can order anything you want to eat, within reason. One portion of my landholding is a farm—it's where we get all our food." He ruffled Rana's hair, earning a squawk of protest.

"I told you so," Rowena laughed, sticking her tongue out at the spell-blade. When Rhyslin ruffled Rana's hair again, Rowena joined in the laughter. "That's what you get for doubting me."

Seeing her chance, Rana pretended to pout. "She's being mean to me," she whimpered, pointing at the seeress.

Rhyslin rolled his eyes, shaking his head. "You are a spell-sword. You can take care of yourself."

Permission enough. Rana slipped from under his arm, darted behind him, and grabbed a fistful of Rowena's nightgown.

"Gotcha," she crowed, dragging the seeress out of his embrace. "You're gonna pay for being mean." Her fingers dove into Rowena's side, merciless in their tickling.

"Hey—stop that!" Rowena laughed helplessly, trying to push her away. Rana's nimble fingers only climbed higher, up the curve of her ribs, to the underside of her breasts. Rowena shrieked and collapsed to the floor, writhing. "Please, for goddess' sake—stop!"

But Rana's grin only grew sharper. Her fingers brushed higher, tweaking Rowena's nipples through the thin fabric of her gown. "That'll teach you to lie to me." She flicked a wicked glance at Rhyslin, who leaned against the wall, jaw tightening.

"You should feel this little bird. She's trembling in my hands. Her nipples are so hard, you can feel them through her clothes." She squeezed, coaxing a whimper and moan from the seeress. "I'll bet she's ready for you to take her here on the floor."

"Rana — Rowena gasped, half-plea, half-protest, as the spell-blade's hand slid lower.

"Shush you," Rana whispered against her throat, lips grazing skin. One hand cupped Rowena's breast, the other pressed down her belly until Rowena arched into the touch.

"Rana, stop — the seeress begged, even as her body betrayed her.

"Oh, you should feel her, Maighstir," Rana purred. She slid her fingers between Rowena's thighs, cupping her heat. Rowena moaned desperately. Rana's grin turned triumphant as she raised damp fingers to her lips and licked them slowly.

Rowena's moan grew into a needy cry when Rana bent close to her ear. "You won't believe how big it is," she whispered, flicking her gaze at the tented cloth of Rhyslin's trousers. "Flur calls it a monster. I'll bet it can't wait to eat you alive."

Rhyslin's eyes narrowed, heat coiling through him, his patience burning thin. "Do you want to consummate your bond now, Rowena — or later tonight?"

All composure fled the seeress. She lifted her head, eyes wild with need. "Now, please, Maighstir. Tha mi a' losgadh."

Without another word, Rhyslin strode forward, scooped her from the floor, and turned toward the nearest door. His voice came as a growl: "If you don't open that door, Rana, I will get you."

The spell-blade's eyes went wide at the raw command, desire mingling with mischief.

She flourished the door open and slipped inside behind him.

Rhyslin laid Rowena on the bed. She reached for him, but his command cracked like thunder: "No—you will not move an inch. Do you understand?"

Rowena nodded, breathless, eyes wide as he stripped his shirt.

"Unless you want to be part of this, you little tease," Rhyslin said without looking at Rana, "I'd run as fast I can."

But Rana could not run. His prana rolled off him like heat from a forge, filling the room, searing desire into the air. She leaned back against the wall, tongue darting across her lips, as she watched Rhyslin strip the seeress bare.

Rowena's body arched beneath his touch, her moans filling the chamber.

Rhyslin's mastery coaxed her from trembling resistance to unrestrained offering, until she yielded utterly.

Rana fanned herself with her hand, her own hunger sharp, as she watched her Maighstir claim his newest bhanna—not just as lover, but as sovereign, as draoidh, as master of her fate.

Chapter Seven

Where Love Blossoms, There Also Lingers Loss

Rana wasn't the only one to fan herself. As Rowena's bond blossomed to life, like a flower straining toward the sun, the very air in the room warmed. Flur's eyes fluttered shut as Rowena's rapture spilled through the link, a rush of heat and brightness that made the lanterns tremble in their sconces.

"You win," she breathed, sliding a piece of fruit toward Ria with hands that shook faintly.

Ria smiled with quiet grace, accepting the cherry and pressing it to her lips. The sweetness burst on her tongue as she asked, "How did you know that he wouldn't wait?"

The brown-haired Hin I-Balanath merely grinned, a spark of triumph in her eyes.

"I heard Rowena and Rana plotting to ambush Rhyslin." She shrugged, her tone playful but edged with wisdom. "It wasn't hard to guess it might backfire, and that he'd answer in kind." She wobbled her hand in a so-so gesture, then added, "I figured it would be spankings for both of them, though him claiming her wasn't out of the question."

Her cheeks flushed as another surge of Rowena's joy swept across the bond, washing through her like a tide. She gasped, fanning her face with her right hand. "Oh my — that was interesting."

When Flur began to rise, Ria reached across the table and caught her hand. The touch steadied both of them, grounding the flood of sensation. "No. Let her savor her first time without us intruding."

Flur's lips parted to protest, but Ria's gaze was firm. "She'll be part of our group soon enough."

Flur pouted, then dissolved into a giggle. "You're right. But oh — it's so tempting to join them."

"You're right about that," Ria admitted with a low chuckle. "I want to barge in there myself. But we must remember: each woman deserves her own time with him." She exhaled slowly, her composure a shield against the waves of heat coursing through the link.

Then her eyes softened. "I do wonder, though — Rowena and Rana conspired together. I cannot help but wonder what my daughter is doing."

Flur tilted her head, squinting as though trying to peer into some hidden current of fate. "I didn't know that. Do you suppose she could be watching them?"

Ria laughed softly, the sound like water over stone.

"If she is, she's red as an apple and wondering how he fit your monster into petite little Rowena." Sliding around the table, she draped an arm around Flur's shoulders, drawing her close. "My poor girl. She's probably learning what mating truly is."

Flur arched one brow, lips twitching with amusement. "That sounded just a little sarcastic." She snickered and rose, stretching languidly. "Let's go outside. Rowena's emotions are about to drown me."

The air around them pulsed in agreement, charged and humming, as though the very walls bore witness to Rowena's joy.

When Ria nodded, Flur led the way to the back door, the two women stepping into the cooler night, the courtyard's stillness washing over them like a balm.

Once in the sunlight, Flur tilted her head back and lifted her face to the sky.

The warmth gilded her skin, and she sighed, "Is it everything you thought it would be?"

"Hmm?" Ria closed her eyes, letting the soft breeze brush her cheeks. The air smelled of roses and sweetgrass, and for a moment she felt as though the world itself meant to soothe her. "Is this everything I thought it would be?" She chuckled faintly, tempted to lie down in the grass and let the day pass her by.

"You know — the mansion, the estate, the servants, all of it."

Ria's lips curved in something bittersweet. "We lived in what I would jokingly call a manor house, but in truth it was little better than an old monastery my people rebuilt. It was drafty and smelled of whatever had died in the walls." Her voice softened, caught between humor and ache. "But it was home for twenty years."

Flur brushed her hair forward over her shoulder, combing it with her fingers. "Why didn't you stay in Mayana's Castle? I know why Mom left and went to *Daingneach ghleann dearg*[2]."

Ria did not answer at once. Her gaze clouded, and the sunlit courtyard seemed to dim with her memory. The air grew still, as though the breeze itself held its breath. "After Garion was killed, I was in so much pain. Maya and Allanagh tried to help me, but I only wanted to run away and hide." A deep breath shuddered through her, and she wiped at her eyes. Through the bond, her voice slipped like a whisper: *[I'm sorry I ruined your day, milis Rowena.]*

What came back nearly crushed her knees to the stones.

---

[2] fortress of the red valley

Warmth, Rowena's seer's fire, Flur's frantic comfort, Rana's shy tenderness, and Rhyslin's steady, anchoring presence. Love wrapped her from all sides until she swayed.

"Oh my, I'm so sorry, Ria. I'm so sorry," Flur cried, dropping to her knees beside her bond-sister and clinging to her hand.

Then the others were there: Rowena, radiant and shaken; Rana, wide-eyed; and Rhyslin, his aura pressing like a shield. Ria was folded into them, a living circle of arms and warmth.

Sensing him most keenly, she threw herself against Rhyslin's chest. "I'm sorry, *Maighstir*, I don't know..." Her words drowned in sobs.

"It's okay, *dh'èirich mo fhasach*[3]," Rhyslin whispered, bowing his forehead to hers.

---

[3] my desert rose that rises again

138

"No, it's not, *Maighstir.*" She wept harder. "I thought I was over it. It's been so long."

The bond trembled, Flur's guilt pricked sharp, and Rhyslin caught her with a raised brow. *[It's not your fault, Mo Dris.]* His thought steadied her, then he turned his whole being to Ria. "It's okay," he murmured, low enough only she could hear. "You don't have to be strong anymore. Let it out."

Ria broke at last, burying her face in him, grief pouring out like a flood. The courtyard air, sweet with blossoms, turned salt-tanged with sorrow as if the world itself wept with her.

"I miss him, Rhyslin. I've missed him for twenty years. I'm always going to miss him."

"I know, Ria. I know." He held her tighter, rocking her against the slow beat of his heart. "I don't want you to forget him. I don't want to replace him. I can't."

He closed his eyes, whispering across the bond: *[Mathair, help me. I don't know what to do.]*

For once, the goddess only poured love, unconditional, unmeasured. It flowed through Rhyslin, into Ria, until her sobs softened.

At last she lifted her head, cupping his chin, searching his eyes. "Do you mean it?"

"Yes." His answer was quiet, steady as stone. "I don't want you ever to forget him. I don't want to be his replacement. I only want you to be happy."

Ria gasped as the weight of his love pressed into her, steady and immovable.

She curled against him again, whispering through tears, "Oh, Rhyslin. *Milis Rowena, I'm so sorry I ruined your special day.*"

But the raven-haired seeress only drew her closer. "It's okay, Mistress. I finally found my home. Any time I get with him is hard-earned and quickly spent—I'll treasure every breath."

Rana had watched as Rhyslin and Rowena had gone from lovemaking to running down the hallway half-clothed in a heartbeat, their bond-fire still shimmering faintly in the air like heat-haze after a storm. She padded after them, barefoot on cool stone, her heart quick with confusion. The taste of ozone lingered in her mouth, the echo of prana spilling down the corridor.

When she caught up, she stood amazed.

Her mother, so often poised, so often untouchable, was folded into a five-way embrace, Ria's sobs spilling raw and unashamed into the bond.

Flur's pulse fluttered like a bird's in Rana's senses, Rowena's newborn link sang like a lyre, and Rhyslin's strength pulsed steady and grounding.

The hallway itself seemed to hush, the morning light filtering through high windows catching like dust motes in holy stillness.

She heard Ria crying and watched as Rhyslin bent close, his voice low and sure, telling her mother it was all right to weep. His prana rolled outward, warm as a hearthfire, loosening the knot Ria had held in her chest for so many years.

Watching him, Rana suddenly understood: this was why her mother wanted to bond with him.

Not for power, not for pride, but for this fierce shelter he gave so freely.

When Ria's grief finally broke and flowed like floodwater, Rana found her feet moving of their own accord. She edged forward, then pressed herself into the circle of arms until she, too, was gathered in. "Momma, why were you crying?" she asked, her voice hushed as though the whole house might be listening.

[What do I tell her?] Ria's question bled through the link, sharp and pained. [She might not understand.]

[You can't treat her like an adult and lie to her,] Rhyslin replied, his tone even, resolute. [If she doesn't understand, she'll let you know.] His presence in the bond was a deep well, steadying.

Ria heaved a soft sigh, her tears damp against Rana's hair, and looked into her daughter's eyes.

The world seemed to hold its breath. "I was mourning Garion's death." Her eyelids fell shut, as if bracing for Rana's questions like blows.

The young spell-blade was silent for a moment, her hazel eyes glinting with the light of unspoken things. "Will you be able to tell me about him? Every time I've asked, you've said no."

"Oh baby." Ria's voice trembled with shame. "I'll tell you anything you want to know." The air stirred faintly around her, as though her vow had weight beyond mere words. Inside, she flinched, had she been a bad mother to keep this wound locked away?

[No, you haven't been,] Rhyslin's voice came like a balm, quiet through the bond. He leaned close, his breath brushing her ear. "I think it's time she knew about him. He was a big part of your life."

Ria closed her eyes, and when she opened them, she carried no evasion, no mask. Only truth. She reached out and pulled Rana close, heart to heart. The bond shimmered between them like water struck by light. "I won't hide anything anymore, Milis Rana."

Chapter Eight

The Lady of Chains and the Web of Night.

Two days had passed since Ria poured her grief into the world, and even now the manor seemed to breathe in quieter rhythms, as though the very stones remembered her sorrow. In the library, the air held the faint musk of vellum and candle-wax, mingling with the ever-present tang of ink. Rhyslin sat in a carved chair, one finger marking his place in the leather-bound tome when a knock, light as a bird's wing, came against the doorframe.

"Yes, Kenna?"

The servant's head peeked around the corner, golden hair spilling over the tips of her feline ears.

She crossed the threshold hesitantly, the quiet tap of her claws against the floor announcing her approach.

Reaching into her pocket, she withdrew a folded envelope and held it out with both hands, reverence plain in her amber eyes. "This came for you, Maighstir."

"Thank you, Kenna."

When Rhyslin accepted it, she lingered a heartbeat longer, tail twitching with unspoken expectation. Only when he raised his hand and rubbed gently between her ears did she melt into a soft purr, winding her tail about his wrist in thanks before scampering away with a trill of contentment.

Her presence left behind a faint trace of warmth and the faintest musk of fur, soon swallowed by the silence of books.

Rhyslin let out a low hum, eyes drifting to the envelope in his hand. The seal broke with a soft crack.

Two sheets slid free, crisp against his fingers. His brow lifted as he scanned the lines, the words brief, but heavy enough to shift the balance of the day.

Meron had woken.

The name seemed to darken the air around him. Without hesitation, he crushed the letter in his fist and cast it into the fireplace. The flames hissed eagerly, devouring paper into ash, the scent of burning wax and parchment curling into the room like bitter incense.

With a shake of his head, he stood. His duster hung from the back of the chair, and when he shrugged it across his shoulders, the leather whispered against his sleeves, settling around him like a mantle of shadow.

At his call, his staff leapt from where it leaned against the shelves, the carved runes along its shaft kindling briefly with light at his touch.

The hallways greeted him with cool stone and the faint echo of his boots. He let his hand drift over one of the etched runes near the head of the staff, voice low and measured. "Rembran, can you hear me?"

The reply was swift, a thread of presence pulled from the ether. "Yes, what can I do for you, Sir?"

For a moment, Rhyslin walked in silence, the air humming faintly with the rune's bond. His thoughts pressed forward to the days ahead, the weight of judgment, the echo of grief still stirring within the house. "Are Ixa and Andros with you?"

"Yes, sir. Andros is outside working some stone, and Ixa is right here with me," Rembran replied. "Do you need us for something?"

The draoidh's lips curved faintly in thought. Rembran's intuition was sharpening, his awareness broadening.

149

Perhaps, in time, he might prove steady enough to train Rana. "Meron is awake and being taken to Talla na Draoidheachd. Ask Ixa and Andros if they want to face Meron in open court."

"You know they want to be there. I don't even have to ask." There was no mistaking the iron in the spellblade's tone. "We'll meet you there."

"Very well," Rhyslin answered. "The council will convene in two hours."

The rune dimmed at his lifted hand, silence falling heavy once more. He let out a quiet sigh and descended the staircase, the tails of his duster brushing against his boots. The air smelled faintly of beeswax and smoke, old house scents wrapped in stillness.

At the foyer's threshold, another voice broke the hush.

"Where are you going, Maighstir?"

He turned. In the shadowed corner, Rana waited, eyes bright against the gloom, her posture taut like a bow half-drawn.

"You seem to have been waiting for me, so I'm guessing Rowena told you where I am going." When she nodded, he flicked two fingers, the motion equal parts dismissal and permission. "Very well, come along if you want to." His eyes caught hers, voice turning edged.

"But you must stay quiet and watch. You are not a voting council member, only a guest."

"Yes, Maighstir," Rana ceded. "It will be as you wish." She slipped from shadow into light, her presence carrying a faint sharpness, like rain about to break.

She trailed him into the courtyard, gaze already turning curious. "How far is it to the Talla na Draoidheacd?"

"The Talla is near Heweston," Rhyslin replied evenly. "And Heweston is nineteen leagues, as the crow flies."

"How are you traveling? By horse?"

He shook his head. "We'd never make it there in time by horseback, and the ship can't be flown until repaired."

Rana blinked at the certainty in his tone. "Then, how shall we travel?"

"By portal." His stride lengthened toward the garden's edge where hawthorn bushes ringed a secluded gazebo. The air seemed to grow colder as they stepped beneath its carved rafters, the bushes whispering faintly as though stirred by more than mere wind.

Rana paused at the threshold, attention caught by the runes carved deep into the obsidian floor. Kneeling, she traced a sigil with her fingertips, the stone faintly vibrating under her touch.

Her voice slipped into the cadence of old Latin, low and reverent. "*Hinc huc illuc Unus gradus ad mille videbimus, De domo in qua, opus esse.*" Hazel eyes narrowed as she puzzled through the words. "Is this a travel spell?"

"Of a sort," Rhyslin said, stepping to the circle's center. The runes along his staff shimmered faintly, answering the deeper pulse within the stone. "It's a matter of intent. When we are ready, I want you to clear your mind and let me take us there."

"Yes, Maighstir." She bowed her head, though her thoughts churned in restless eddies. Clearing her mind felt like asking the sea to still its waves.

The air of the gazebo thickened, as if awaiting command.

The hawthorn's blossoms stirred faintly though no breeze moved them, their fragrance sharp and otherworldly, heralding the path soon to be torn between worlds.

"Yes, Maighstir," Rana bowed her head, wondering how she was supposed to clear her mind when it was full of busy thoughts.

Rhyslin closed his eyes as he stood in the circle's center, the staff humming faintly in his hand. The air grew taut, charged, as though the world itself were holding its breath. A low vibration spread through the obsidian under their feet, deep as a heartbeat, and Rana's balance faltered. Instinctively she moved to Rhyslin's side, clutching her arms as if to steady herself.

He raised his right hand, and threads of silver fire wove through the air, tracing four runes that burned briefly before dissolving into shadow.

The scent of iron and wet stone filled Rana's nose, and her ears rang with a hollow chime.

When the portal opened, it was like a tear in the air, shadows bending inward, whispering with unseen voices.

Rhyslin stepped forward without hesitation, swallowed by darkness. Without being told, Rana followed, the chill of the void brushing her skin like cold water. When light bloomed again, she found herself on another obsidian dais ringed with hawthorn. The branches rattled though no wind stirred, as if recognizing who had crossed their threshold.

Rana arched her left eyebrow at him, suspicion mingling with awe, but Rhyslin only returned her look with calm assurance. She grinned despite herself and trailed him past the thorny hedge, where an unadorned building rose from the field.

"Is this the Talla na Draoidheachd?"

Rhyslin nodded. "You were expecting something grander and more befitting a mage's council chamber?"

When she nodded, his mouth curved in quiet amusement. "We saved the grandeur for the *colaiste draoidheachd.* [4]The Talla is where we conduct business, hold trials, and sentence the guilty to their dooms."

A shiver traced Rana's spine, and she rubbed her arms against the sudden chill. The ground itself seemed to quiet around them.

The silence broke with a crack of thunder as a lightning portal ripped open on the dais behind. Sparks scorched the air, and Rembran emerged with Ixa and Andros at his side.

---

[4] College of Magic

The smell of ozone lingered as the three stepped down. Rembran inclined his head in a half-bow.

"Did we make it in time?"

Rhyslin nodded. Ixa clutched Rembran's arm, eyes searching.

"Is it true? Did Meron awaken?"

Another nod made her tremble. "What if he lies?" Her voice was small, almost lost against the weight of the place.

"He won't be able to lie. Lady Ananke won't allow it, nor will Quetzalcoatl." Rhyslin gestured to the entryway, where faint golden runes stirred and pulsed as if answering his words. "Come along, it's almost time."

Inside, the Talla greeted them with hushed grandeur. The foyer exhaled a cool breath of air that smelled faintly of rain and dust. Luminescent sigils crawled along the walls like living veins of light, their glow shifting as the group entered.

Floating orbs drifted in the chamber's corners, casting steady illumination that pulsed faintly in rhythm with Rhyslin's steps.

Rana's breath caught. The high-backed chair at the rear loomed like a shadowed sentinel, its black leather gleaming as if polished by judgment itself. Around the central dais, empty seats awaited their masters. So far, only the storm and fire *maighstirean* had arrived, their presence like twin tempests, crackling energy and restrained heat.

Rhyslin pointed to a bench along the southern wall. "You can sit there and wait until Meron is brought in. Then, as each of you are called for, approach the bench, give your testimony, and answer any questions asked."

As the four seated themselves, he crossed the floor to the waiting mages. "Thank you for coming. I hate that it had to be for such a dire reason."

The storm mage tilted her head with a half-grin, blue-black hair catching the orb light. "It's been a while, Maighstir Darkblade. I, too, wish it could be under better circumstances." She brushed her hair back with deliberate grace, her eyes bright with unspoken challenge.

"Best be careful," the fire mage teased, a rough chuckle escaping him. "Word has it Maighstir Darkblade has bonded three women in the last three weeks. A careless gesture, and he could do the same to you." He dipped his head respectfully toward Rhyslin.

Rhyslin's answer was calm, but his staff flared faintly as he nodded. The storm mage stiffened, eyes widening.

"Three women? Truly?"

"Yes, three. And if my *ciad-bhanna* has her way, I'll bond more and more, until my house is full."

The storm mage colored faintly and turned away, her composure cracking for just a heartbeat. But before she could respond, footsteps echoed through the chamber.

Rana turned and saw Meron being escorted in, flanked by a spell-blade, a cadaverous necromancer whose presence chilled the air, and an earth mage whose very steps made the stone tremble faintly. Shadows recoiled from the necromancer's touch, and the scent of loam and dust marked the earth mage's wake.

"I had best take my place," Rhyslin murmured, dipping his head before mounting the dais.

When he sat in the high-backed chair, the runes flared brighter, acknowledging his authority.

The spell-blade stamped his right foot three times, each strike ringing like a bell through the stone. "The prisoner has been brought forth to be judged according to the precepts handed down by the gods."

Rhyslin lifted his right hand, his voice ringing with solemn finality. "This court takes charge of your prisoner and will hold him until the truth is known."

The air thickened; the orbs dimmed for an instant before blazing back with renewed brilliance.

"So, mote it be," the spell-blade intoned, pushing Meron forward.

The spellblade's voice rang like steel in the chamber. "Sit down, traitor." His stance made it clear that if Meron did not obey, he would be driven to the stone by force.

"No — I think not." Meron's words carried a chill that bled into the vaulted air, cold as the void itself.

As he stepped to one side, the chains at his wrists groaned. His eyes gleamed as he lifted his arms in a grandiose gesture.

"Sszyrrakh!"

The sound scraped through the Talla like spider-silk strung too tight. To Rhyslin's ears, the word bent wrong against the order of creation. The chamber shuddered. Runes along the walls guttered as if choking on shadow, and the light-orbs flickered, dimming toward gray.

With a hiss, the manacles cracked and fell from Meron's wrists, striking sparks as they struck the stone. He turned, his black gaze fastening on Ixa and Andros.

"LaiIxaArias, SerAndrosFerrasPulmos, to my side now!"

The syllables cut like hooks. For an instant, the air around the elementals trembled. Dust lifted at Ixa's feet, rising as if to spiral into chains.

When neither moved, Meron's lips thinned to a knife's edge. "Ixa — Andros — to my side now, or I will punish you."

Upon hearing her soul-name spoken aloud, Ixa shot to her feet, trembling with fury. "No! — I will not obey. I am no longer bound to you."

The dust at her feet did not coil into shackles, but instead swirled upward in defiance, a rising storm that rattled the sigils overhead. At her side, Andros stood rooted, the stone beneath his boots humming faintly, unshaken by fear.

Meron's face twisted in disdain as he turned his focus to where Rhyslin already stood, staff leveled at his heart.

"I don't know how you broke my bonding, but it means nothing." He kicked the chains toward the spellblade, and sparks skittered across the floor like fireflies made vicious.

A voice like braided song and judgment came from behind the spellblade: "I broke the false bond, thou knave. May I have permission to enter your hall, Mac Draoidheachd?"

The air thickened, and Rhyslin tilted his head slightly, memory stirring. He knew that voice. He drew a steady breath. "You may, Our Lady of Chains."

The heavy odor of frankincense and myrrh spilled into the Talla, sanctifying the air. The runes steadied, the orbs flared with soft gold, and a spiraled portal unfurled in light. From its depths stepped Ananke.

Her sky-blue chiton shimmered with stars that spun slowly across its border, as though the heavens themselves bent to her garment.

Her sandals made no sound upon the stone, yet the hall seemed to bow in silence at her presence.

She crossed the chamber without haste, her gaze calm, her bearing unassailable. When she reached Rhyslin, she inclined her head in formal benediction. "Thank you, Mac Draoidheachd."

Her lips curled, echoing Meron's disdain. The air itself seemed to tighten at her words, as if chains unseen coiled around the chamber.

"Your binding was cruel, inhumane, and not worthy of a Saorsan Magus." Her eyes bore into Meron's, the faint glimmer of stars flickering in their depths. "You violated the law and intruded upon my station."

If she meant to frighten him, the magus didn't show it. The shadows around him seemed to lean closer, gathering at his shoulders like a cloak.

"Poor goddess, angry that a mortal dared intrude upon her sacred ground."

His laugh rang bitter, as sharp and hollow as ice cracking on the northern seas.

Ananke faltered. His absolute lack of fear was wrong, alien. She stared at him as one might a spider crawling across a holy text, fascinated and repulsed all at once.

"What foul being has corrupted your soul?"

"Fouled my soul?" Meron's smile was slow, venomous. "Freedom cannot be foul, Our Lady of Chains." His tongue flicked the title into mockery, dripping contempt.

Rhyslin took one deliberate step forward, staff humming faintly with restrained draoidheachd. The floor shivered as if eager for violence.

"No, no, no." The black-robed mage wagged a finger, his voice suddenly intimate and poisonous. "Step closer and I will kill you, old friend." He practically spat the endearment. "You have my word on it."

Before Rhyslin could answer, the spellblade raised his sword, steel gleaming with stormlight.

"What can you do, unarmed?" His stance was iron, the blade angled toward Meron's throat.

"Khrethzzar."

The word slithered from Meron's lips like silk spun in the rafters. At once, invisible cords snapped tight around the spellblade's limbs.

He froze mid-step, muscles straining, jaw locked. His breath came ragged through clenched teeth.

Meron moved past him with leisurely cruelty. "Unarmed? I don't need artifacts to project my will, boy." He stepped in close, palm flashing out to deliver a derisive slap across the cheek. The sound cracked in the vaulted chamber, echoing like a whip.

His black eyes glittered with an oily sheen as he turned back to Rhyslin.

"Don't come after me, old friend. I don't want to have to kill you." The warning was quiet, all the more chilling for its certainty.

Rhyslin's staff burned faintly brighter, his voice cold.

"You'll never be able to set foot in the Saorsa again, Meron."

The temperature in the Talla plummeted. Breath misted in the air.

Meron laughed, head shaking slowly, almost pityingly.

"Who will stop me, old friend? You can't even stop me from leaving."

He raised his hand. Lines of shadow etched themselves in the air, spinning outward in radial patterns until a vast spiderweb hung where Ananke's portal had been.

The strands pulsed faintly, dripping in darkness.

"Chryzzhka." The word thrummed like mandibles clashing. Webs thickened across the threshold, blotting out starlight with veils of black silk. The faint sound of chitinous legs scraping echoed in the minds of those who watched.

Meron bowed mockingly, a courtier in some grotesque parody of ceremony.

"I'll take what's mine and be gone, old friend. When next you see me, I will be marching across your pitiful border with allies the likes of which you've never seen."

Then, without a backward glance, he stepped into the webbed darkness and was gone. The threads shivered once, then stilled, leaving behind a silence heavy as a tomb.

Chapter Nine
The Summons of the Web-Lord

"Chryzzhka."

The portal peeled open like a torn web, spilling into the lower level of a squat, square mage tower buried deep in the Saorsa, not far from Oak Grove. The Magi's robes whispered in the dark, rustling like many-legged things, and his eyes, already altered, drank in the blackness.

He strode to the center of the chamber and pressed his palm against the crystal set into the table. "Kael-Surae Vael." At his command, the crystal flared, and pale light spilled outward, bright enough to reveal the table, the scattered books, and the cobwebs sagging from the rafters. To any other eyes, the room would have remained a void. *{I have returned, my loves.}*

Almost at once, the stair-door groaned open above, and two young women came sprinting down. *"When did you get home? Where have you been?"*

"Ssivath — nai'shrae."

The words slid through the chamber like silk. At once the women fell quiet, gazes fastened on him, trembling with excitement and expectation.

"We have to leave soon," Meron said, priming them with his urgency. "The Draoidh disrupted my plan. They took me to the *Talia na Draoidheachd* and put me on trial." Two pairs of eyes blinked in perfect unison, and warm thoughts brushed against him, delicate as spiders crossing a leaf. "Yes, yes. I escaped — and came to get you."

It was a testament to their training that neither asked a question. They knew he would explain in time.

"Fetch our get-away bags. Tell the soldiers to be ready within two hours. The magisterium will not take long to follow my trail."

{Of course, my love,} said the first, a slight woman with long black hair. She nodded once, then fled back up the stairs; rallying the soldiers was her charge.

{I'll return in a moment,} said the second, a shade older, her white hair gleaming in the glow. She leaned close, brushed her lips across his cheek, and then slipped away to gather their packs.

When the last footstep had faded, silence pressed against the walls. The air in the squat chamber grew heavy, thick with the musk of damp stone and the faint sweetness of rot. Meron bowed his head, eyes closing, as he let his mind fall open to the chaos.

{Where have you been, Meronkae?}
The voice of his master crawled through him, not only in thought but in the twitch of his skin, as if unseen legs had brushed across his scalp. {You didn't answer the summons. I had to bring despair and death into this realm to look for you.}

Meron did not bother to frame an apology. His will unlatched, and he bared his memories like raw flesh for the god to feed upon. He could almost hear the skittering of countless limbs, feel threads pulling through his veins as the one he knew only as The Spider read him like a book.

{It is unfortunate that you were disabled by the shock,} the god said at last, his tone cool, detached. {A shame you lost the elementals, but it could not be helped.}

Meron shivered despite himself. He had never once heard of The Spider losing his temper.

That patience, measured, inexorable, was worse than rage. It meant a prey might not even notice the fangs until they pierced bone.

{It wasn't a total failure.} His lips barely moved, though his thought carried clearly into the web. {Given time, I can force shrythraen on others, and the accursed oathbinder cannot see them.} He would not grovel. If The Spider wished him dead, silk would tighten, and he would die.

The silence stretched—then came a low, rolling chuckle, like threads thrummed in a vast darkness. {Good. We can use that.} The voice recoiled, leaving an emptiness colder than stone. Then it returned, sharp as a fang. {Take your brood and find Saldren. He'll have a place for you.}

Meron's eyes opened. The chamber seemed dimmer; the torchlight swallowed by shadow.

A slow, dangerous smile curved his lips, brittle as glass. He could not wait to meet the half-drake.

A quick look to the right found his women kneeling at his side, while five soldiers stood behind them, eyes downcast as though caught in a web. Arrayed behind the white-haired woman were three packs, sealed in silk and set precisely in a row, always ready to grab and carry.

When he brushed his fingers across the back of her skull, she tilted her head and beamed with joy, like a moth quivering at the touch of the spider's thread. Her master was pleased with her.

Meron nodded at the dark-haired woman, who smirked faintly, her gaze glimmering with the promise of glorious rewards later. Turning his attention to the soldiers, he reached into their minds and tugged the strands of thought, implanting the instructions to gather the rest of his men and make their way beyond the border between Bazan and Ghaliende to search for the half-drake.

The five men, without blinking, raised their hands in brisk salutes. Their movements were too perfectly in sync, as though pulled by invisible filaments, then they slipped out in silence to gather their squads. In the grand scheme of things,

Thirty-one soldiers weren't a grand army, but Meron had stripped the fear from their minds. Bound to him by threads they could not see, they would hunt down his enemies without hesitation, either killing them or dying in the attempt.

When the last soldier had gone, Meron signaled for his bonds to shoulder their packs while he cinched his own.

He had first taken these women for beauty and for devotion to a god older than memory, a god who sat in a net high above Crann Na Beatha, raining chaos along his sticky strands.

The thought pulled him back to the night of the ceremony. He smelled resin smoke burning in a cracked bowl, sharp and bitter. His fingers had bled onto woven cords, the blood soaking into the floor as he traced the pattern the old scrolls described. The air had thickened, trembling like a web in wind, and then a voice had come, many voices, whispering as one.

{Not heaven. Not reward. But chaos. Be my hand in the world. Free me, and the strands will shake kingdoms.}

He remembered the way his knees had struck stone, not in fear but in awe.

He had promised his life, the lives of his bonds, his fortune, all of it. That vow had bound him more tightly than any spell he had ever cast.

Now, years later, his scalp prickled with the phantom brush of spider legs. He had not forgotten. The time to shake the world was at hand.

The dark-haired woman lifted her eyes. *{To where do we travel?}* It was not idle curiosity but practicality, destination dictated dress, demeanor, and how deep their deceit must run.

He understood that well. "Our soldiers have their mission, and we have ours." His smile was slow, shadowed. "We are to find Death and Despair and take them to a place where they can recruit more soldiers for our god."

The fair-haired woman, ever clever, canted her head toward him.

179

Her pale braid brushed her shoulder as she studied the night sky through half-lidded eyes.

{How do you think the guardian will react to our intrusion?}

Meron's chuckle carried through the chill like metal striking stone. Frost drifted from his breath, curling against the air before vanishing.

"He will react as he always reacts," he said, the mirth in his tone both weary and cruel. "But he will see the wisdom of our god's ways."

She nodded once, calm as snowfall, and waited for her master to set them on their way.

Meron looked up into the Crannic sky, its indigo depths pulsing faintly as if aware of his gaze.

His eyes traced the constellation that formed the spider, the eight limbs spun wide across the firmament, and the twin stars of its eyes fixed unblinking upon a single point of the world below.

Once, this place had been a temple to the spider-god. Now its pyramid lay broken, ribs of stone jutting through vines and frost. The webbed portal had cast Meron and his bonds into the courtyard, where snow mingled with dust and half-buried bones.

He wasted no time. Kneeling amid the ruin, he opened a pouch of sacred salt. The grains hissed faintly as they met the cold earth, releasing a dry, mineral scent that stung the air. He poured them in slow spirals, forming concentric circles laced with runes that crawled and shifted like living script.

A grim smile curved his lips. The night itself seemed to hold its breath as he turned from the stars and walked to the circle's heart. There he knelt and laid a shattered mirror upon the ground—its edges catching moonlight in cruel, broken lines.

"Oh, great world-shaker, I seek your sight."

He drew a cobweb from his sleeve, delicate as breath, and stretched it across the mirror's face. The strands quivered as though alive.

"Oh great spider, I come to your call."

He raised the mirror toward the heavens, the web trembling in his grasp, and tilted it to catch the moonlight. A thin beam spilled over the ruin, refracting into silver threads that danced along the fractured stone.

"As a pebble along the shore, I seek Despair and I seek Death."

His voice deepened, roughened, as he began to rock back and forth. The light on the mirror's face shimmered, flickered, then seemed to move of its own accord, tracing ghostly webs upon the temple's fallen walls.

"I call out to your greater servants," he whispered. "May they come to us."

He set the mirror down with reverent care and leaned back upon his heels. Around him, the air thickened, soundless, heavy, waiting.

{Now, we wait.}

At his side, his two bonds bowed their heads, eyes fixed upon the sky's unblinking stars. Neither dared speak.

The frost beneath them began to web outward from the circle's edge, forming fine crystalline strands across the stone.

{All praise to the world-shaker.}

Death and Despair, the ultimate predators, lingered in stillness, biding their time as they waited to hear back from their patron.

The wind had long since died in this place. Only the whisper of falling ash moved through the ruins, dry, soundless, eternal. Death, the great skelletdrach, lay curled as he had in life, an immense coil of fossilized bone and iron-black scale, his form half-buried in snow and time. Frost clung to the hollows of his ribs, glittering faintly in the pallid light that filtered through the shattered towers of the ancient keep.

Leaning against the ridged curve of Death's spine sat Despair, still as carved obsidian. His armor was tarnished by age and battle, the once-golden filigree now dulled to soot and shadow. The cold flame in his helm's eye slits burned low, pulsing faintly like a heartbeat that refused to die.

Since that day when they had come across the great airship, crewed by mortals touched by divine power, the two had withdrawn into silence. They moved unseen beneath the gaze of Nan Diathan and their Taghte, burying themselves beneath the layers of the world's notice.

It was Death who had found the place they now occupied: a courtyard scorched by an ancient war, where the ground still bore the scent of brimstone and the echo of screams long silenced. Nothing grew here.

The stones were blackened and fused, the well long dry, and the shadows clung like cobwebs spun by forgotten gods.

Death had tested the air, the faint shimmer of his nostrils drawing in the cold, and when he was sure no living thing dared dwell within the keep's shadow, they had claimed it as their lair.

To mortal eyes, the passage of days would have been unbearable. The silence, the cold, the emptiness would have driven any heart to madness. But Death and Despair were not mortal. They sank into a deathless stasis, a twilight of awareness where time meant nothing. Thought dimmed to embers, motion ceased. Only instinct, that ancient, preternatural sense for danger or command, remained awake beneath the frost.

And so they waited.

They waited as the snow fell in soft waves, burying the courtyard inch by inch. They waited until the ruin looked less like a fortress and more like a tomb.

Two slow weeks passed before the stillness broke.

The skelletdrach's wings, half-shattered bones stretched beneath frozen membrane, stirred with a sound like cracking ice.

186

The snow that had gathered across his body cascaded down his flanks in a shimmering avalanche. Fragments of frost glinted as they fell, scattering the faint light like shards of glass.

Despair's head lifted, the faint glow of his eyes brightening within the helm.

The ancient dragon shook himself, bones clattering softly in the cold, and dipped his massive skull toward the armored figure beside him. His voice came not as sound but as resonance, a thought that reverberated through the marrow of the dead earth.

{Are you awake, old friend?}

The massive helm inclined, shedding flakes of frost. When he rose, the movement was deliberate, almost ceremonial, as though waking were an act of will.

{What task does the ancient one have for us?}

The flames in his eyes flickered like twin candles struggling against a storm. He brushed snow from his shoulders, an unnecessary gesture, but one that spoke of old habit, old pride.

The snow would never freeze him, nor could the cold harm what no longer lived. Yet he preferred to meet his god unburdened.

The still air trembled faintly around them, a prelude, perhaps, to the coming command.

The first motion in two weeks came as a tremor through the courtyard, a faint shiver that stirred the snow piled on Death's flanks. The *skelletdrach* lifted his skull, vertebrae grinding softly in the still air. Frost cascaded from his horns, scattering into the darkness like splinters of pale glass.

Above, the night was a vault of ink and starlight. Clouds drifted sluggishly, torn and frayed by the wind's distant touch. Somewhere beyond them, high and terrible, shimmered the faint glint of a thousand eyes woven in a single web, the constellation known to few mortals, but to Death unmistakable. The spider in the sky was watching.

Death raised his head fully and turned his snout toward those burning eyes. His long, black tongue flicked once in acknowledgment, tasting the pulse of divinity on the air. His posture shifted, attentive, listening, though no mortal ear could have caught the whisper that crawled from the heavens. For a long moment he was perfectly still, his hollow chest filling with silence.

When he finally turned his gaze downward, the green glow in his eyes was no longer dull.

189

It had deepened into something virulent, alive. The light leaked from the sockets in thin ribbons, painting the snow in ghostly hues.

{The spider wants us to go pick up his convert.}

The mental voice rippled through the air like laughter breaking beneath ice, dry, cold, and faintly amused.

{Apparently he has a tale to tell, and an offer to make.}

Despair straightened, brushing the frost from his shoulders. The armor creaked as he moved, shedding ice in quiet flakes that glimmered briefly before fading into the gloom. The cold flame in his eyes flared once, steady and resolved.

{Then, by all means, let's go pick up the convert.}

He turned toward Death's massive side and climbed with practiced ease, gauntleted hands finding holds in the bony ridges as if guided by long memory. The air seemed to tense around him, the silence before a storm.

When he reached the saddle hollow between the dragon's ruined wings, he seated himself with soldierly precision. The haft of his lance gleamed faintly in the dying starlight.

When he was ready, he lifted the weapon in salute, not to Death, nor to the heavens, but to the unseen will that bound them both. Then he leaned forward, his voice firm.

He urged the skelletdrach into the air.

Death spread his wings, each one a cathedral of bone and shadow. The air around him buckled with the force of old magic awakening.

He didn't *need* to do this, the draoidheachd that animated his corpse could have borne him aloft in utter stillness, but even death could not unlearn the habits of life.

With a sound like distant thunder, his wings cut through the night.

The first beat sent a shockwave through the courtyard. Snow and ash spiraled upward in a maelstrom of silver dust. The keep's blackened stones quivered under the pressure of his ascent, and the world below seemed to exhale, as if relieved to see him gone.

Death circled the lair twice, a ritual more than a necessity, each revolution marking a vast ring of displaced mist that caught the faint, green gleam of his eyes. Below, Despair's lance burned faintly like a cold star.

Then, with one last beat of his tattered wings, the *skelletdrach* shot southward, an arrow of bone and shadow, vanishing into the horizon where snow met cloud.

The storm swallowed them whole, but long after they were gone, the sound of their departure echoed through the ruin like the tolling of a buried bell.

Chapter Ten
The Courtyard of the Unliving

Drawn by the prayers of their god and guided by the pale illumination of the tracking device, Death and Despair traveled unceasingly toward their destination.

The sky stretched endless and black above them, a frozen sea pricked with starlight. Death flew higher than any living creature could dream of, higher than the mountain peaks, higher than the breath of storms. The wind no longer touched him; air itself seemed to shun the cold bones that carved their way through its thin currents. His vast skeletal wings stirred the void with a sound like cracking ice, though no mortal ear could have heard it.

Far below, the world lay drowned in shadow, rivers like threads of dull silver, forests reduced to tangled ink.

Even the clouds looked lifeless, a gray shroud spread over the wastelands. From this height, the earth seemed distant, unimportant, a forgotten corpse beneath the stars.

Perched between the shattered ridges of his mount's spine, Despair rode motionless, his armor rimed with frost. The cold flame within his helm burned steady and dim, casting only the faintest glimmer upon the black metal of his gauntlets. He did not speak. He did not need to. The bond between the Todesriter and the Skeletdrach was older than memory, older than speech. The rhythm of their flight, the slow rise and fall, the tilt of wings through invisible air, was conversation enough.

They did not tire. They did not breathe. The mortal concept of distance meant nothing to them.

What others crossed in weeks, they traversed in hours, passing above snow-drowned plains and mountain ruins half-buried by time.

Only the twin stars that marked the eyes of the dark constellation followed their every move. Cold and unwavering, those lights burned with an intelligence that was not of the world. Wherever Death turned his skull, he could feel their gaze, vast, patient, ancient. They were not stars at all but the eyes of the Spider, watching from his throne beyond the veil.

And far below, in the wastelands that still remembered the sound of divine war, a ruin stirred.

The temple waited there, squat and crumbling, half-sunk into the ashen soil. Its stones were veined with frost, its altar broken by time and neglect.

The banners that once bore the Spider's sigil had long since rotted away, leaving only tatters that whispered faintly in the dead air. It was a place forgotten by mortals, but not by gods.

From the safety of a deep cavern, the newly freed Spider-God and his priestess watched through a pool of water as the two skeletal servants approached the ruin.

And high above, Death banked, descending toward the broken temple, silent as falling ash.

{Look down, my friend,} Death whispered as they circled the ancient temple. {It is one of his old haunts—and people are gathered in the courtyard.}

{So I see.} Despair inclined his helm, the cold flame in his eyes flaring faintly as he looked down upon the three figures below.

They stood in the center of a cracked courtyard, enclosed within a glowing circle etched into the frozen stone. {Let us introduce ourselves and see if they are worthy of his attention.}

The skelettdrache angled his descent. The motion was vast, deliberate, each beat of his tattered wings displacing the air with thunder that no mortal ear could quite hear. Ancient, weathered leather stretched between bone and shadow; runes long eroded flickered faintly across his frame like dying stars.

Below, snow and ash swirled in spirals as he came down through the clouded air.

His breath, if breath it could be called, shimmered in the cold, wisps of emerald mist curling from his fanged maw.

He struck the earth with the authority of something that had once been a god's weapon.

The impact cracked the flagstones, sending spiderweb fractures racing outward across the courtyard. The night shuddered with the echo. As always, he was preceded by the drachenfurcht, the primeval dread that walked before him like a herald. It seeped through stone and marrow alike, an unholy pressure that bent the air.

But the mortals did not flee.

Neither scream nor gasp rose from the three within the circle. The two women kneeling behind the man trembled, but not in fear. Their eyes gleamed with awe, their lips parted in something perilously close to delight.

Death tilted his massive skull, hollow sockets burning with pale green fire. The gesture was ancient, reptilian, a predator's curiosity. He extended the drachenfurcht over the kneeling figures, testing them as a storm might test the shore.

199

Still, they did not move. The air grew colder, the silence deeper, as snowflakes settled between the dragon's ribs.

{Maighstir, the great ones have arrived.} The dark-haired woman's voice broke the stillness, calm and reverent, carrying the ease of long habit. Her words drew Meron from his dark meditation like a thread tugged free from shadow.

{Should we run screaming around the courtyard?} the fair-haired woman asked, her tone almost playful, a soft ripple in the solemn air.

Meron merely shook his head, rising with a slow grace that spoke of confidence earned through corruption. He turned to face the ancient pair, his expression unreadable beneath the frost-streaked light.

{I guess not,} the fair-haired woman murmured, feigning a pout before she and her bond-sister rose in unison.

They circled behind Meron, silent as moonlight, the rhythm of their motion ritualized, practiced, a dance as old as devotion.

When their formation inverted, the triangle complete, Meron bowed deeply. His bond-mates mirrored him, offering the ancient courtesies with perfect stillness. They could have held the pose until death itself claimed them, if that had been their master's wish.

The courtyard lay still in the wake of the dragon's descent. The air itself seemed stunned, vibrating faintly with the echo of its landing. Dust and ash drifted in slow spirals through the green glow of Death's gaze, settling like snowfall upon broken stone.

No one moved. Even the wind held its breath. The smell of iron and frost mingled in the silence, the scent of endings.

The two women knelt as if carved from the same marble that littered the ruins, their cloaks stirring only when the skeletal dragon exhaled a mist that shimmered like ghostlight.

Meron's head remained bowed. The weight of divinity pressed against his will, testing its seams, but he held his posture. His heart beat, once, a single, deliberate thud that sounded too loud in his own ears.

For an instant, he allowed himself to feel the enormity of what he had summoned. Then, with a slow, measured breath, the Magus raised his chin and let composure flow back into his voice.

"Welcome, oh great ones," Meron said, his voice smooth as oil over ice. "I am Meron, known to the great spider as Meronkea."

The women did not so much as twitch.

The wind tugged at their cloaks, and the sigils on their collars glowed faintly beneath the temple's dying light, but they remained as statues, perfect, obedient, divine.

A cold wind swept across the courtyard, stirring dust and snow alike. The skelettdrache folded his wings inward, the vast bones creaking like ancient doors, and lowered himself until his skull loomed level with the mortals.

The light of his eyes deepened, casting spectral green across the broken stones.

{You resisted my drachenfurcht. I am impressed.}

The voice thrummed through the ground itself, through marrow and metal, resonant and immense. The sound was not merely heard,it was *felt*, like the deep toll of a buried bell.

The women lowered their gazes in reverence. Meron's smile flickered, sharp and thin, as frost drifted from his breath.

Despair stepped out of Death's shadow, the air warping around him as if recoiling from the sudden weight of his presence. The already weak moonshine dimmed, torches guttered, and the black marble stones reflected his shape only in distortion.

A faint smell of ash and decay accompanied him, curling through the cold. He set his burning eyes on the magus.

"You, I can understand, as Magi can harden their will."

Those eyes of flame drifted over the two women standing rigid beside Meron. Their skin gleamed with an unnatural pallor, and their pupils did not so much as tremble. Even the fog that crept through the hall seemed to hesitate before touching them.

"How did you make them immune to fear?"

"My lord Despair." He offered a bow at the waist, his robe whispering like dry leaves. "I have taken their fear and bound their wills to mine." The frosty smile widened into one of macabre glee. "I would have had others, but there was interference."

"Who dared interfere with The Great Spider's plans?"

The air trembled faintly at the title. Somewhere above, the faint scraping of chitin on stone suggested their unseen master's attention. Despair's flames guttered lower, fascinated less by the women now than by the scent of defiance that clung to Meron's words.

Meron shrugged, feigning indifference though his jaw twitched with restrained fury.

The candles around him hissed as his power pulsed. "By the ancient nature goddess, the Mac Draoidheacd, and the accursed goddess of chains."

Death turned his helm toward him, a motion that drew a frostline in the air. His voice came like ice cracking on a frozen lake.

"Explain. The Spider himself listens."

Meron's lips peeled back in a silent snarl. The air around his staff shimmered faintly, reacting to his spite. "I had two elementals in my power and ready to present to our master, when a storm bolt summoned up the accursed nature goddess rendered me unconscious." He drew on his store of patience and continued through clenched teeth. "During that time, Mac Draoidheacd and the accursed goddess of chains worked together to break my hold."

If he could have, Meron would have killed Rhyslin and Ananke on the spot, their names burned like acid behind his eyes. The temperature in the hall dropped another degree, frost crawling along the walls.

The Todesritter raised a gauntleted hand, the motion, stiff and deliberate, and stroked the base of his helm, a ghost of a gesture from a life long extinguished.

"Can it be done to others?" Despair inquired, his voice more curiosity than threat, though the shadows themselves seemed to lean closer at the question.

Meron drew a slow breath that sounded almost like a hiss. "It can. In fact, I have almost thirty soldiers that are under my control. Their wills are mine, as are my bond-mates."

The Todesritter gave a hollow laugh that echoed like a coffin lid closing. "Where are your soldiers, Meronkae?"

The magus bobbed his head slightly. The torchlight danced across his pale face like moving scars. "On their way to find the Half-Drake and join his army. They will follow his commands until they are reunited with me."

Death lifted his head to the heavens and listened. The whisper of many legs filled the air, a susurrus of threads spinning somewhere beyond mortal reach.

"Our Lord is pleased to hear about your procedure. Do you have anything else to offer us?"

The sound of spinning silk faded, replaced by the hollow hush of anticipation. Meron shared a look with his bond-mates, and all three nodded as one, perfectly synchronized, eerily calm.

"I do. I have an army for our lord. One that you two will appreciate."

Freezing mist coiled up from the floor and enfolded them, veiling their forms in a shroud of pale smoke. The stench of old graves lingered within it. Death cocked his head, the motion slow, deliberate.

"How did you find an army that would serve our lord?"

Meron laughed — a deep, resonant sound that seemed to shake dust from the rafters. His eyes gleamed like twin coals as the mist thickened.

"What can our lord do with an army of the unliving?"

The Skelletdrache leaned down, grave dust falling from decayed fangs. The movement stirred the air, carrying with it the scent of rusted metal and long-dried marrow. Bone scraped faintly against stone as its ribs expanded with a breath it no longer needed.

Shadows twisted across the walls, shivering in the cold phosphorescence that bled from its hollow eyes.

"Unliving? Explain it to me. How does a world that has a soul-wheel have unliving beings?"

Meron drew himself up to his full height and behaved like he was teaching an unruly student. His robes whispered as he moved, a faint static shimmer of enchantment in the seams. The torchlight caught in the crystal rings that hung from his fingers, scattering fractured light across his face like splintered halos.

"The Great Wheel of souls isn't infallible. If you have sufficiently powered intellect and soul, you need not be reincarnated." He gestured to Despair. "You could for instance, store your soul somewhere the gods can't dig it out."

Death looked at Despair, and the two shared a look, one that spoke of disbelief. The silence between them was not empty, it pulsed faintly, as if the air itself recoiled. The faint hiss of drifting ash filled the pause. Despair turned his head toward Meron. "You mean there are beings like us, here on this world?"

"Of course I do." Meron commented. "A whole necropolis full of them."

For a brief moment, the drachenfurcht vanished completely, as if it didn't exist; even the sound of its presence—the soft grind of bone, the wheeze of empty lungs—flickered out. Then Death pulled back his head and stared at the magi. The torches dimmed in the wake of his motion, their flames bowing inward as though to avoid his gaze.

"Can you take us to them?"

Meron's smirk went unnoticed. His eyes gleamed like a cut of obsidian in the half-light.

"I can. When would you like to go?"

Death reared his head back and looked down at the magi. "Now. At this moment." The drachenfurcht spiked, sending shivers down the women's backs.

Meron chuckled low in his throat. "I don't have a problem with that. Just let us mount up and we'll be ready to go."

This was the point it could all fall apart. All if would take was Death remembering he was a dragon-lich for the whole thing to crash.

The skelletdrache lowered itself just enough for the women to climb onto its back and settle in behind where Meron would sit.

Hiding his victory behind a false smile, Meron climbed up and took a place in front of his women, but behind Despair, who climbed back into his saddle.

"Hold on tight. It's going to be a fast trip." Despair ordered as he leaned back in his saddle. "Think of the place and Death can find it."

Chapter Eleven
Beneath the Black Star

In the span of a heartbeat, Death had taken flight and circled the spider's temple. Frost streamed from his ribs like ribbons of smoke, and the night groaned beneath the weight of his wings. Each beat sent tremors through the air—slow, ponderous, the sound of glaciers shifting in the dark. Below, the courtyard lay shattered and still, the remnants of the banners whispering against broken stone.

{Where is this necropolis?} the skellettdrache rumbled.

The voice rolled across the sky like a collapsing mountain. Even the clouds shuddered; flakes of dead snow spiraled upward instead of down, caught in the pulse of the dragon's passing.

{It would be easier to show you than tell you.} Meron leaned toward Despair, his cloak dragging frost from the wind. A thin crust of ice glittered across his armor where the dragon's breath had touched it. {Is there a way we can make that happen?}

The Todesritter would have smirked if he still had flesh and blood. Instead, a faint creak issued from his helm, the sound of iron remembering what it once was. The spider's tracker had served its purpose and could be retasked to serve another. He reached into his side pouch—metal scraping softly against metal—and drew out the crystal. The gem pulsed faintly in his gauntlet, its inner light the color of drowned stars.

{Take this and think about your necropolis.}

He handed it to Meron. The magus accepted it with reverent precision, his breath clouding the air in slow, measured curls.

The gem's surface was cold enough to burn. He closed his fingers around it and lowered his gaze, the faint glow staining his pallid skin green.

He thought about where the hidden city lay buried beneath the world—its gates sealed with runes, its streets paved in bone. He thought of who dwelled there and what ancient guardians watched over its silence. The wind around them fell still, as if listening.

When he opened his eyes, the gem was softly strobing. One facet shimmered with a gentle, verdant light, and the entire crystal seemed to orient itself—pointing, unwavering, toward the direction he would lead the skellettdrache.

{Here. It should do the trick.} he said, handing the gem back to Despair.

The Todesritter accepted it without a word. The pale flame within his helm brightened for an instant, casting long shadows across Death's skeletal flanks. Far below, the temple's ruined altar gleamed under the flicker, and the faint echo of silk stirring—perhaps from the Spider's unseen web—passed through the cold air like a sigh.

Despair watched the tracker as they circled the temple, then directed Death.

{Take us west. The tracker is pointing towards the mountains.} When they started off on the correct direction, he amended. {Don't go too high, our passengers won't survive the extreme cold at altitude.}

The skelletdrache's laugh resonated through the sky, changing the direction of the drifting snow.

The ground below blurred into ghostly streaks of gray and white as Death, under Despair's silent guidance, cut through the freezing air toward the distant, jagged wall of the Ghaliende Mountains. The peaks loomed ahead like the spines of a slumbering god, their crowns veiled in stormcloud and snow. The wind keened against Death's bones, a voice without warmth, hissing through the seams of his armor as though trying to find what little life remained within him.

{Just so you know, these mountains are home to the Hin I-Balanath people. They don't tolerate strangers in their mountains.} The fair-haired bond whispered.

{Hin I -Balanath?} the Todesritter inquired. {I have never heard of this race. Tell me about them.}

The fair-haired bond turned her lips up in a partial snarl, though her tone remained flat. {The Hin I-Balanath were the first people on Crann na Beatha to see the sunlight. They can be very beautiful or handsome, and they are powerful magi and unrelenting soldiers.} Were it not for the fact that Meron had stolen her fear, she would be jealous.

Below them, the mountains unfurled, a labyrinth of ice and shadow. Frost-rimed forests crouched in the valleys, and rivers, frozen mid-flow, gleamed like veins of glass. Here and there, black crags jutted from the snowfields, their shapes like fangs biting into the low clouds.

Death looked down upon the range, the ghostlight in his hollow eyes reflecting silver across the endless drifts. {And they call these mountains home?}

He'd never admit to being afraid, but curiosity had always been a weakness of his. Choosing prudence over risk, he gained altitude, climbing through the thinner air until the wind screamed around his wings like knives.

Despair listened impassively to the explanation, the flames in his eyesockets flaring, painting streaks of dull red against the cold gray air. {Do any other beings live in these mountains?}

{Oh, very much so.} Meron replied. {The Clann na h-Oidhche and Clann an Dorchadais live in and around those mountains.}

As his thought rippled through their shared link, a shadow passed beneath them, a tangle of cliff and cavern that seemed to breathe.

Even the wind changed there, thickening with a faint metallic tang, as though the stones themselves remembered blood.

Instead of asking Meron about these races, Death dipped into his mind, drawing rough impressions from his memory. The visions came disjointed but vivid, wolfkin and shifters beneath a pale moon, Infernals whose eyes burned like forge-fire, and shapes that blurred the line between flesh and spirit.

{I take it that neither of the two groups are native to this world.} the skelletdrache commented.

{You're correct.} Meron replied. {Both came from other worlds. The accursed nature goddess invited them to stay.}

A silence fell, colder than the mountain air. Even the wind seemed to falter, its wail dropping to a low hum that trembled along Death's wings.

The air grew dense with unseen weight, the awareness of old powers still awake beneath the ice.

Cold that had nothing to do with the weather clung to the two outworlders. What had they stumbled onto?

As those thought percolated through his mind, Despair watched as Death effortlessly cut through the mountains, ignoring the hin I-Balanath keeps, the Infernal nests, and the shifter enclaves. He kept glancing down at the converted tracker, which kept pointing at one particular mountain. The tallest, darkest looking mountain that seemed to have no life save trees and underbrush.

Reaching out with his senses showed an absence of intelligent life, with animals being in abundance.

After five long hours of skirting the cold perimeter of hin I-Balanath strongholds and passing the silent villages of hin I-dorchadas and oidhche, *Death* descended through the veils of mist and snow. The *skelletdrache*'s wings whispered like torn silk as he landed at the base of a black granite mountain. Frost cracked beneath the sweep of his talons, sending up a thin mist of powdered ice.

The air here was heavy with magic, stale, metallic, and old.

The *drache* lifted his skull-crowned head and inhaled, frost gathering around the cavities of his ribs. His hollow eyes flickered briefly with blue fire.

{This is a powerful warding spell. What does it do?}

His mental voice was as cold and slow as the glacier beneath them.

Meron dropped lightly from the drache's shoulder, his boots sinking into the crusted snow. The wind cut across his face, sharp with the scent of stone and sorcery. He approached the jagged wall where the air shimmered faintly, runes glimmering like veins beneath ice.

"It hides a door," he murmured, brushing frost from the surface.

Despair dismounted next, steadying the two *bonds* as they clambered down. The sound of their boots, *crunch, crack, crunch,* echoed softly against the mountainside.

{Why would anyone hide a door?}

he asked, curiosity threading through the bleak air.

Meron traced a sigil with a fingertip, leaving behind a faint trail of silver light.

{So the very gods themselves can't find you,} he replied, voice low and distant.

His hand trembled slightly as he completed the rune, a spidery glyph that seemed to crawl beneath the stone.

The mountain shuddered in answer. Ice fell in sheets from its face, breaking apart like glass. Acting under the compulsion of his working, the warded surface began to twist and recede. A seam split open, revealing a massive doorway, tall enough for the *skelletdrache* to pass through. The darkness within was absolute, swallowing even the glimmer of runelight.

Meron turned, the faint glow of his magic reflecting in his eyes.

"Are you ready to meet your army?"

He drew a final rune in the air. The mark hung for a heartbeat, then sank into the stone.

The doorway groaned and slowly parted, exhaling a gust of air that smelled of iron, dust, and centuries of silence.

Before them yawned a tunnel that led into the mountain's heart, black as the void, waiting

Death tilted his skull toward Meron.

{Our army lives in the darkness?}

His gaze followed the tunnel's vanishing throat, a corridor of stone and silence where even echoes refused to return.

{They do,} Meron replied, inclining his head. {Of what use is light to the unliving?}

Despair nodded slowly, his breath misting in the cold air.

{The unliving don't need light — but what of you, and your bonds?}

Meron's lips curved into a faint smirk. He turned to his companions.

"We don't need light, do we, *Mo luaidhean?*"

The two women stepped forward, their hands resting lightly on his shoulders.

"Of course not, my master," the fair-haired one murmured, voice soft as velvet. "We can see perfectly well in the dark," the dark-haired one added. "Our god has provided that for us."

A faint tremor rippled through the mountain. Death inhaled, and the stale air tasted of rust, cold stone, and forgotten blood.

{This draoidheachd is very old. Does it predate the arrival of the gods?}

Meron shook his head.

{No, though it predates the wheel by a short time.}

His voice was almost consumed by the darkness as he turned, gesturing to his bonds. They followed him into the blackness without hesitation.

Despair came next, the fire of his armor flickering across the stone like a heartbeat.

After a long pause, Death folded his tattered wings close and entered the tunnel. The ground trembled beneath his weight. but even so, he was careful not to crush the fragile lives before him.

Death paused for a moment as the hidden door silently closed behind him.

Their success or failure would determine whether or not they saw the surface again.

Meron led the way, sure of foot and steady of gait. He had visited this place once before, and as it had every day since then, the power called to him.

His two bonds almost skipped as they followed in his footsteps, neither the darkness nor the cryptcold bothering them.

The Todesritter paused as he sensed something familiar. He raised on hand, resting it above a sigil carved into the rock. {I know this symbol.} He said, breaking the silence.

The skelletdrache extended it's neck and examined the strange sigil. {It's a supplication to Chaos.}

{It is indeed,} Meron agreed. {In this case, to prevent the wheel from taking hold of the souls that herein reside.} The sigil reflected in his eyes, eldritch lines of force dancing across the black pupils.

Death reached out with its senses, the air around him humming with ancient resonance. {There are others down this passageway.}

Meron nodded into the darkness. {Indeed there are and they are older than I've ever encountered.}

With the ancient draoidheacd a guide, the quintet walked deeper into darkness, Death and Despair pausing every so often to examine the sigils carved deep into the stone.

At the end of the long tunnel, they came to another door, this one guarded.

{You have returned, living one and you have brought oherssss.}

The voice coiled into their thoughts like smoke through cracks.

{You were warned about ever coming back here.}

Meron halted, sweeping into a low, deliberate bow.

{I am aware of that, oh great guardian. I have defied your order,} he drew himself to his full height and gestured behind him. {I bear a message from the spider-god.}

{Ooooh, doooo youuuu?} The voice sounded amused, as if such proclamations were made every day, and with each lofty speech, meant nothing. {And what messssssage does the World-Sssssshaker have for us?}

{He is once again on his web, and with him rides chaos.} Meron answered, his eyes dancing with the eldritch lines from the sigils.

{I am not alone, old guardian.} He calmly said, peering into the darkness, as if he could see the speaker.

{Do you think that you can ssssstop me from killing you and your bondsssss?} The voice asked, as scaled digits slithered across the cold stones.

Before Meron could answer, Despair stepped up beside him. {Meronkae might not be able to stop you, but I'll wager that we can.}

The creature behind the voice laughed scornfully. {Can you now, Todesritter?} The sound of claws being dragged across stone echoed down the passageway. {Do you know how many of your kind I've devoured?}

Despair canted his head to the left, his eyes blazing. {There are very few like me and even fewer who serve the great spider.}

{Neverthelesssss, even you would be hard pressssed to stop me.} the voice stated in a chilling tone.

{And myself, Wyrm?} Death inquired, releasing the barest trace of drachenfurcht, not scare to unliving, but to remind it of its status. {Do you think that you can destroy me?}

The creature hissed as it sensed the skelletdrache. It drew itself to it's full height and stretched its shadow wings to the limit. When Death didn't move, it slithered closer and looked up at the massive skelletdrache. {You, I cannot defeat. What does the great spider call you?}

{Death!} The skelletdrache replied, stretching its neck down to stare into the creature's eyes.

The creature lowered itself to the ground, not in defeat, but reverence. {This one is Macraww, Guardian of Long sleep. How may we serve the great sssspider?}

{Grant us entry into Long Sleep,} Death intoned. His ribcage expanded as if drawing in air he no longer needed, then contracted again, a gesture of breath without life.

{It sssshall be assss you wissssh,} the voice replied reverently. The guardian withdrew to the doorway and traced a talon across the sigil.

Stones shifted with the sound of grinding ages. Beyond the threshold, the door opened upon an immense cavern.

{Come thissss way. Long Sssssssleep welcomessss you,} the voice whispered, receding into the vastness.

The quintet followed and stopped at the brink.

Below them sprawled Long Sleep, the city of the Dead.

Under a black star that shed no light, the necropolis stretched into infinity: towers of bone, crypts carved from basalt, vaults veined with cold fire. Rivers of pale mist wound through graveyards like forgotten breath.

Death stepped through the archway and looked down at Macraww. The unliving wyvern lay prostrate, wings spread across the stone like a shroud, head bowed low.

{My Lord Death,}

the guardian murmured,

{below you lies the Necropolis of Long Sleep.}

Meron nodded, contented by what he saw. {You should be rewarded for your faith.}

The air around them shimmered with the faint reek of sulfur and scorched stone.

Ash drifted down like slow snow, clinging to the magi's robes and the scales of the great wyvern beside him.

Macraww tilted his head to one side, his tongue flicking. {And how would you do that, Living man?}

The creature's breath came out in thin, misty ribbons that coiled over the cracked earth. Beneath its talons, the ground trembled faintly, a reminder that even the calmest wyvern was a heartbeat from violence.

The magi grinned as he swept an exaggerated bow. {If the guardian will permit me.}

When the wyvern bobbed its head, Meron stepped a pace apart.

The sound of his boots grinding over shattered glass filled the silence as he drew from his satchel a cracked mirror and a web clinging to a frame of bone.

He placed them reverently on the ground, his hands steady despite the tremor in the air.

"Great spider who strides the sky, great weaver who webs on high. Your faithful are gathered here to see just a small part of your self appear."

Those gathered around him had to strain to hear his prayer, the wind had gone sharp and thin, whistling through the ruins as if reluctant to bear the words. The cobweb glistened with cold dew, trembling as if alive. Then the mirror brightened, suffused with the same impossible light that burned in the black sun above them, a radiance without warmth, casting shadows where it touched.

They stepped back in reverence as a black-robed figure rose soundlessly from the mirror's surface. The air thickened; the ground moaned beneath their feet.

"Meronkae, you have done well," the figure stated as it set its red eyes on the Magi. "You have found my army."

An emaciated hand reached up and drew back the hood, revealing the face of the spider god, a visage stretched and angular, eyes like molten rubies caught in webbing of night. Threads of darkness trailed from its limbs, tethering it to the reflection below.

"Chaos will spring from this place and spread across the world like a great wave."

The god turned its attention to Death and Despair, who stood like twin statues, motionless, expectant. "You have, as usual, exceeded my expectations. Take some time and rest here. I will send for you when I need you to do something."

As the last words fell, the air seemed to exhale.

The mirror dulled to gray, and the strange radiance faded, leaving only the low hum of the wyvern's breath and the echo of something vast retreating into silence.

Chapter Twelve
The Sundering of the Web

"You'll never be able to set foot in the Saorsa again, Meron."

Rhyslin's staff burned faintly brighter, its runes bleeding pale fire into the air. His voice was cold enough to frost the edges of each word.

The temperature in the Talla plummeted. Breath misted and hung like ghosts between the pillars. The faint warmth of the torches guttered, their flames stretching thin and blue before winking out entirely. The marble floor, veined with silver, caught the chill and shimmered as frost crawled outward from the dais.

Meron laughed softly, the sound brittle and distant, as though echoing from the depths of a tomb. He shook his head slowly, almost pityingly.

"Who will stop me, old friend? You can't even stop me from leaving."

He raised his hand. The shadows obeyed, rippling outward like spilled ink. Lines of darkness etched themselves into the air, spinning in perfect radial symmetry until a vast spiderweb hung where Ananke's portal had once glowed. The strands pulsed faintly, oozing drops of liquid night that hissed where they struck the frozen floor.

"Chryzzhka."

The word thrummed through the Talla, resonating like mandibles clashing just beyond sight.

The web thickened across the threshold, blotting out starlight with layers of black silk. A faint, alien sound followed, the whisper of chitinous legs scraping across stone, echoing not in the ears but in the minds of those who watched.

Meron bowed low, mockingly graceful, a courtier performing in some grotesque parody of ceremony.

"I'll take what's mine and be gone, old friend. When next you see me, I will be marching across your pitiful border with allies the likes of which you've never seen."

He stepped into the webbed darkness without a backward glance. The strands rippled, shivering once before stilling. The woven shadow hardened, then faded, leaving only silence, a silence so heavy it pressed against the ribs, swallowing even the memory of sound.

Even before the last flicker of the portal's light had vanished, Rembran and the Talia's Spellblade had their swords drawn. The steel caught what little light remained, flaring briefly as they charged toward the place where Meron had stood moments before.

Both Rhyslin and the chief Magister called out at once.

"Rembran, stop!"

"Beyun, Halt!"

Rembran turned on Rhyslin. "But sir, we can — " He froze when he saw the look on Rhyslin's face, the shock, the disbelief, and the sorrow barely held in check. The magister had already stepped between the fading portal and Ananke, his staff still glowing faintly at his side.

Rhyslin shook his head. "No — we can't. We don't know where that portal leads." The Draoidh's voice softened, weary and low, as if the world itself leaned against his shoulders. The light on his staff dimmed to embers. "Relax, Lieutenant, we'll chase Meron down later."

He turned toward Ananke, noticing for the first time the leaf-bladed sword in her hand.

242

The weapon gleamed with argent light before dissolving into drifting motes that swirled like fireflies in a winter wind.

"Are you well, M'Lady?"

"I am well, Mac Draoidheachd, only surprised by the depth of your magi's treason."

Her voice was smooth, controlled, but the air around her rippled with restrained power. As she lowered her hand, the last of the motes faded.

"That language he spoke. I think it was tied to an ancient spider god who was recently released from Claiginn." She brushed a strand of hair back from her face, her expression grave. "Did you have any clue as to his true loyalties?"

Rhyslin shook his head. "No, I was just as surprised as you were. This Talia has stood for almost three hundred years, and nobody has ever escaped justice."

He glanced at Rembran, who stood rigid, his knuckles white on his blade.

Would you have time to tell me more about this spider god?"

The goddess shook her head. "I must confer with someone before I divulge that information." She traced a sigil through the air, each motion leaving a trail of faint golden light. The shape bloomed into a spiral portal, its edges rimmed in the shimmer of a thousand turning stars. "If I can get permission, would you have a problem visiting us?"

Rhyslin dipped into a half-bow, his breath still visible in the cold. "I would be honored, Our Lady of Chains."

For a moment, Ananke's expression softened. A warm, radiant smile, brief as dawnlight, touched her lips before she stepped through the portal and vanished.

The Talla was left in silence once more. Frost reclaimed the floor, the torches still dead, and in the far corner where the web had once hung, a faint line of darkness remained, a scar in the air that refused to fade.

The air inside the Talla still carried the aftertaste of divinity, cold, metallic, and faintly electric. Frost clung to the marble floor in pale veins, and the torches lining the walls sputtered weakly, their flames still reeling from the goddess's departure. Every breath hung visible in the chill.

Rana had come with Rhyslin expecting to see routine justice dispensed upon a treacherous criminal. Never in a million years had she expected to see that criminal break his chains, mock a goddess, and threaten her new home with invasion. She didn't know what to think about it.

Looking to her left, she saw the shock frozen on Ixa's face and the resigned heaviness in Andros' expression. Even they, veterans of Rhyslin's circle, looked undone by what they'd witnessed.

Her world, once no larger than the desert and her mother's house, had grown vast and strange. The people Rhyslin called friends, had welcomed her as one of their own, patient and kind. Now, seeing pain twist their faces, she felt it like a bruise inside her chest. She didn't know how to comfort them, or if she even had the right.

Pushing off the bench, she brushed nonexistent wrinkles from her skirt, a nervous habit more than a need, and walked toward Rhyslin. The marble was slick beneath her boots, the frost whispering as it broke. He stood with his staff still faintly glowing, prana curling around him like mist.

She hesitated, then reached out and tugged gently on his sleeve.

Rhyslin, who had felt her approach through the ripple of her aura, turned slightly. His prana still swept the chamber in slow, tidal waves.

"What do you think, *mo phrìseil?*"

Rana's mouth opened, but no words came at first. Her thoughts churned like wind through dry sand, scattered and directionless.

"I expected to see justice carried out, not a prisoner escape." She tried to keep her tone even, she didn't want to offend him, not when she'd only just begun to feel at ease here.

She was slightly startled when Rhyslin turned fully toward her. The glow from his staff softened the hard lines of his face.

"You heard what I told Ananke — about how old the Talla is?"

When Rana nodded, he continued.

"Never in all our years have we had a prisoner break the iron shackles or escape us." His right hand crossed to pat hers. "Never you fear, we'll find Meron, and whoever is helping him."

The warmth of his hand steadied her. She smiled faintly and leaned against him for a moment, the lingering cold forgotten.

"What are we going to do now?"

"That is a good question. With Meron's escape, I need to inform the council and prepare the appropriate defenses."

His voice carried a weight that seemed to fill the hall. Around them, the frost crackled faintly, the sound of a structure remembering its purpose.

Outside, the wind moaned through the arches, and the faint scent of ozone still lingered where the goddess's portal had been.

Rana looked at the pale breath rising from their lips and thought, not for the first time, that the world had grown much larger than she had ever imagined, and infinitely colder.

The echo of departing footsteps still haunted the Talla, carried on air that shimmered faintly with the residue of divine power. The great hall felt colder now, the kind of chill that crept into the bones and settled there. Frost spidered through cracks in the marble floor, catching the dim light from the hanging lamps and scattering it into shards of pallid color.

Leaving Rana to her thoughts, Rhyslin turned and walked toward the other magi. Each step was slow, deliberate, the stride of a man who had carried too many burdens for too long.

His staff tapped against the stone with a soft, rhythmic echo, a heartbeat in the silence.

"Ilara, can I depend upon you to inform the members of the Talla, the Colaiste Draoidheachd, and the military?"

Ilara straightened, the light glinting off the silver threads in her robe. For a moment, her face was unreadable, the professional mask of one accustomed to crisis, but her eyes betrayed a flicker of grief. "Of course. I take it you are going to report to the council."

When he nodded, she lowered her gaze, shaking her head slightly. The faint motion sent the edge of her hood stirring, like a sigh given form. "It hurts when one of our own betrays us."

"That is true," Rhyslin said quietly, the words heavy as lead. He inclined his head, then turned and made his way back toward his people.

The sound of his footsteps faded slowly, swallowed by the vastness of the chamber. Around them, the remnants of spellwork still hummed, faint, spectral vibrations that rose from the stone like the echo of a storm long passed. Ilara watched him go, one hand resting against the cool surface of a pillar, and whispered a prayer that the gods no longer seemed inclined to hear.

Upon reaching his people, he softly said, "Let's go. Home is calling." He led the way to the travel circle and then had them all gather around. "I think it would be easier to go to Am Flur Manse and let you stay the night."

He glanced at the two elementals. "If you have time tomorrow, I'd like to speak with the two of you."

Ixa stepped to Rembran's side. "Can Maighstir Rembran come along?" she asked, verifying what Ria had said about the elemental's relationship with the spell blade.

Rhyslin nodded, "Of course, he can. If you've bonded with him, it would be wrong not to." The faint blush on Ixa's face further confirmed this.

"Of course, Maighstir. We'd be honored to stay the night at your Saor-Shelh and meet you in the morning."

"Then it is settled," Rhyslin nodded. "Let's get home." He reached the circle's center and tapped the staff against the stones.

"Hinc huc illuc Mille gradus ut videmus Accipe nos ex hoc loco Domum videre volumus.[5]"   As before, the portal opened. Rhyslin gestured for the group to precede him into the darkness.

Rembran, Ixa, and Andros stepped out of the shadowy portal and turned to thank Rhyslin for helping them, only to find out he and Rana were nowhere to be found.

"Where is he?" Andros stalked around the circle where the portal had been.

"You don't suppose they went somewhere else, did you?" Ixa inquired as she clung to Rembran.

The spell-blade shook his head. "Rhyslin wouldn't do that. At least not without telling us about it."

---

[5] From here to there A thousand steps as we see Take us from this place To the home we wish to see.

Ixa eyed the spot where the portal had been, "Do you think he's okay?"

"There's only one way to find out," Rembran said as he approached the house. "His bannaichean can tell us if he's okay." Upon reaching the front door, he raised his right hand and placed it on the sigil set into the center of the door. A long tolling sound echoed in the foyer.

Rembran waited a few minutes, then began raising his hand again, pausing only when the door opened. Ria smiled as she saw who was outside.

"Rembran, what brings you here?" the fhasiach bhanna inquired as she fully opened the door and invited them inside.

Rembran chuckled, "Oddly enough, we were traveling back from the Talla Na Draidheachd with Rhyslin and Rana, and when we arrived here, they disappeared."

"Disappeared?" Ria threw him a curious look. "In what way?"

"When we stepped through the portal, it closed, and neither Rhyslin nor Rana were here." Ixa took a step toward Ria. "We were hoping you could tell us if they are okay."

"Oh, I see," Ria smiled as she closed her eyes, sinking into the bond. "Hmm, wherever he is, he is not in danger." She blinked and looked at Rembran. "If anything, he's slightly amused by something." Then she chuckled. "Rana's with him, or he'd be worried."

"At least he's okay," Andros commented, offering a half bow. "Before he disappeared, he invited us to spend the night and talk to him about something in the morning."

The raven-haired Hin I-Balanath nodded once. "We'd be honored to have you stay the night. Please follow me."

Chapter Thirteen
The Hall of Silent Light

The world dissolved into silver mist. Rhyslin, walking at the back of the line to ensure everyone returned home safely, felt the familiar hum of prana shift, a ripple of wrongness that crawled along the edges of his perception. He reached forward to steady the current, only to watch Rembran, Ixa, and Andros vanish into the ether as if swallowed by fog.

A quick glance at Rana brought a flicker of pride. The young woman had already stepped back toward him, her hand resting lightly on her sword's hilt, her stance steady and sure. The light of the portal caught her hair and the edge of her blade, both glinting with pale fire.

Rhyslin covered her offside with half a step, instinctive and silent. When she met his eyes, he nodded toward the faint glow ahead, the proverbial light at the end of the tunnel.

Rana's chin lifted slightly in response, her body coiled and ready.

She moved forward, quiet as a shadow, and peered through the veil. The light spilled across her face in strange gradients, neither warm nor cold, but colorless, like sunlight seen through water.

When she stepped back, her expression was puzzled. "It's not home."

It said much about her adaptability that she called *Am Flur Manse* "home" after only three days. Rhyslin gestured for her to continue, his curiosity tempered by caution.

"It looks like some ancient place," she whispered, "all columns and pillars and artwork that would make momma jealous."

She hesitated, her brow furrowing. "The light is weird. There are no shadows except for a few places where there's smoke."

Rhyslin already suspected where they were. His pulse quickened, not with fear, but with recognition. He gave a small nod and motioned her forward. Rana swallowed once, squared her shoulders, and stepped through the light.

The air on the other side was cool and dry, filled with a faint metallic tang like air trapped within a sealed tomb. Rhyslin followed close behind her.

They stood in a vast chamber that seemed to breathe. Marble columns soared upward, veined with faint gold that pulsed softly, as if alive. The floor was carved from single slabs of translucent stone, each one etched with spirals that shifted underfoot when viewed from the corner of the eye.

The light came from nowhere, diffuse, directionless, filling every corner without casting a single shadow. Where shadows *did* exist, they curled like smoke, writhing in place before vanishing.

Rhyslin stepped up behind Rana and laid a reassuring hand on her shoulder. "There is no threat here unless we bring it with us."

"If you say so, maighstir." Her voice was steady, but the tension in her shoulders betrayed her unease. Her gaze swept the vast hall, watching the way the air seemed to ripple as if the world itself breathed.

Rhyslin walked toward a long table at the chamber's center. It appeared to have been carved from a single massive tree trunk, smooth, warm to the touch, its surface swirling with intricate spiral patterns that mirrored the designs on the columns.

The scent of cedar and something floral, perhaps divine incense, hung faintly in the air. He traced a fingertip across the polished grain, noting the faint prana hum beneath it.

"Inviting guests into your home and then hiding behind the curtains is considered impolite," he said, his tone light, but his eyes sharp as he brushed his hand across a crystal decanter filled with a silvery liquid that shimmered like quicksilver.

The silence that followed was deep enough to feel. It pressed against the eardrums, filled the chest, the stillness before revelation.

Then, movement.

Two figures emerged from behind a veil of golden light that shimmered near the far wall.

The first was Ananke. She had shed her armor and severity, her dark hair now falling loose to her mid-back.

The white wrap dress she wore gleamed faintly, like woven starlight. Her presence softened the air itself.

"You are right, Mac Draoidheachd," she said, her tone even but laced with contrition. "It was rude not to greet you in person." Her gaze met his, calm, assessing, and reverent. For a heartbeat she felt an almost physical urge to kneel. *Astinmah had not exaggerated,* she thought. *He truly could be a diathan.* "I ask forgiveness."

"Lady Ananke," Rhyslin half-nodded. "There is nothing to forgive." His attention shifted to Rana, who was trembling now, her wide eyes darting between the goddess and the still-shimmering veil. "Who's our other host?"

Ananke lowered her gaze, a faint smile flickering at the corner of her lips. "You can come out, Despoina. I don't think Mac Draoidheachd will hurt us."

"I think I'm just going to sit down over here," Rana muttered, nearly collapsing into a chair. The furniture felt solid and warm, humming faintly under her palms like living wood.

Rhyslin glanced around the chamber, scanning for the goddess of mysteries.

"What should I do?" came a voice like wind whispering through silk. "I can't. I don't. I'm at a loss for what to do. The future is unclear."

Rhyslin's lips quirked slightly. *So even the Seeress can be blind.* "It would be inhospitable of me to hurt those who have invited me into their houses."

Despoina emerged slowly, her movements hesitant. Her black eyes were wide, searching, her dark hair falling around her like a veil. She moved with the careful grace of someone stepping across thin ice.

263

"How do mortals live this way," she asked softly, voice trembling with wonder, "unable to see the future?"

"It is the only way we know," Rana said, her voice barely above a whisper. Her awe tempered her fear. "We never know the future." She tilted her head, curiosity overcoming hesitation. "How do you do it — knowing everything ahead of time?" She frowned slightly. "Do the other gods know every second of the future?"

Rhyslin shrugged, his expression faintly amused. "Maybe not as far into the future as she does." He gestured toward Despoina, whose entire body tensed at the motion before she cautiously seated herself across from him. "Can you see the destiny of the other diathan?"

Despoina's gaze fixed on him, intense and searching. "To an extent. I can see enough of it to interact with them."

She reached forward, her cool hand brushing his forearm as though to test that he was real. "You are the only person I can't see. It's so odd — I can't even see people standing near you."

Rhyslin lifted an eyebrow. "What about Ananke? She's sitting across the table."

"She's my sister," Despoina replied, blinking slowly. "I can see her." Her gaze drifted toward Rana. "I can see Vuuroena." Then back to him. "But you — I can't see at all."

He couldn't resist teasing. "Am I here if you can't see me?"

Despoina pouted, the divine veneer cracking into something almost human. "You are mean, Mac Draoidheachd." She pinched his arm lightly, the gesture oddly intimate for a goddess.

Rhyslin's laughter was soft, a ripple in the quiet hall. He placed his open hand over hers. "If I may — why did you bring us here?"

The chamber shimmered with faint, unsteady light, a soft gold that seemed to pulse from the air itself. Columns of translucent stone rose like frozen waves, their surfaces veined with silver and pale green light.

The scent of ozone and old parchment mingled, the atmosphere charged with the quiet weight of divinity.

The two goddesses exchanged a glance. The air between them shimmered faintly, a current of silent communication passing like light through water. Finally, Ananke cleared her throat and met his eyes.

"We brought you here to talk about the spider-god."

Rhyslin leaned forward, boots whispering against the polished floor, and made a 'Tell me more' gesture. The faint rustle of his coat seemed to echo unnaturally in the stillness. Ananke and Despoina leaned toward him, their divine radiance casting subtle halos that flickered like reflections on rippling glass.

Ananke reached into the ether and pulled out a set of elegant-looking keys, their silver edges humming with restrained power, a sound just at the edge of hearing. Despoina duplicated the gesture, revealing hers to be iron skeleton keys whose weight seemed to draw warmth from the room.

"We are keys. It is our task to monitor the gods that are locked up in Clagainn."

Rhyslin brushed his hand across his neatly trimmed beard as he watched the two goddesses, his gaze moving between the glinting keys.

"Clagainn? The infamous Skullcap — the prison of the gods, and you are what, judges, jury, jailors?"

Despoina glanced over at Ananke, then back to Rhyslin. The faintest shimmer of frostlight danced across her cheek.

"Administrators — would be the most precise term. We are supposed to admit the gods who have committed crimes to Clagainn, then monitor their prison term, and if needed, release them." She looked down, traces of red dancing across her cheeks.

Rhyslin couldn't tell if it was from embarrassment or anger. The air around them tightened, a low hum rippling through the chamber as if it, too, awaited judgment.

The Draoidh examined what little he knew before hazarding a guess. "This spider god —"

"Iktomi," Ananke whispered.

268

"This spider god," Rhyslin wasn't about to name a strange god in a place that he didn't own. "He escaped from Clagainn."

Despoina shook her head slowly. Her braids shifted, catching faint glimmers of divine light. "We don't think he escaped." She paused, her tone softening. "We think he gained enough followers to be released."

Where Quetzalcoatl would have demanded answers, and Huitzilopochtli would have growled, Rhyslin simply watched the two goddesses, his silence deliberate, the kind that carried weight. A faint draft curled through the chamber, stirring the edges of his cloak as if to remind them all of the living world beyond.

"What did this spider god do to be imprisoned?" He expected tales of blood and ruin, a deity of war or corruption, not mere mischief.

When the goddess of bonds whispered,
"He was a chaotic disruptor. He was
imprisoned by his brother and father."
Rhyslin blinked and tapped his right ear.
"I must have heard you wrong — he was a
chaotic disruptor?" He couldn't fathom such
a god being locked up.

"That's correct," Despoina softly replied.

"That's hardly a crime," Rhyslin
retorted, exhaling a slow breath that fogged
faintly in the cold air of the sanctum. "Even
for nan diathan." He sighed. "Most of the
troublemakers in the old empire could have
been considered chaotic disruptors. We
didn't lock them away."

"We know this, Mac Draoidheachd,"
Despoina said, tugging the end of her hair in
distress. The movement sent a faint shimmer
of gold through her tresses. "We didn't put
him there, but he's come to Crann Na
Beatha and we aren't sure what he's up to."

Rhyslin wasn't about to tell a pair of goddesses that they had failed in their tasks. The air tasted faintly metallic, divine tension building like the charge before a storm. Before Despoina could yank her hair out, Rhyslin caught and held her hands. Her skin was cool, like polished marble warmed by candlelight.

"What's in the past is in the past. Who is the sagart that got him released?"

Despoina froze at his touch. "The akashic records said a priestess by the name of Brigid Augustdotir got him released." She wondered if he could feel her heart beating faster.

"I don't know a priestess named Brigid, but if memory serves, there was talk about a draoidh candidate several years ago who completed her training in four spheres of power."

He saw the pout on Ananke's face and released Despoina's hand. "Is this all you wanted to talk about?"

Despoina shook her head, her hair catching faint motes of ethereal light that drifted like embers. "No, Mac Draoidheachd, we — I wanted to talk to you about Vuuroena."

The chamber seemed to darken at that name, as though the walls themselves had drawn a long, quiet breath.

"What about me?" Rana perked up, hearing her name spoken. Her restlessness gone, she joined the three at the table.

"You are changing her Destiny," Despoina's eyes fixed upon Rhyslin's face.

The draoidh met her gaze. "For better or for worse?" He sounded concerned. He wanted her to survive, but not at the cost of changing her completely.

The diviner reached out and took Rana's hand. "It changes, and every day that she's with you, it changes more." She seemed at a loss for words.

Rhyslin leaned forward, placing his hand on Despoina's cheek. "I know it's not my place, but I'd like to know how it's changing," he said.

Despoina drew in a ragged breath at his touch. "Before she moved in with you, I kept seeing her die while freeing captives held by a being of chaos. Now, I see her survive, but her spirit and body are torn asunder." She closed her eyes. "I believe that the longer she stays with you, the higher her chances of survival."

She leaned into Rhyslin's touch. "Do you intend to bond with her?"

Rhyslin was silent for a moment. He had discussed this with Rana, and both had agreed to wait until she was older and her destiny fulfilled. "In the fullness of time, I do."

Despoina looked at Rana and half-nodded. "I see. Teach her to survive, Mac Draoidheachd. She'll need it."

"She'll be ready," Rhyslin promised. "The rest will be up to her."

At his side, Rana shivered as the weight of her doom settled on her. She promised herself that she would do whatever she could to help others.

With the main reason for the visit over, the four settled into a long discussion about the women Rhyslin had already bonded with. Ananke laughed when Rana told the story about Rowena's bonding and her mother's actions.

"It's not fair that they made me promise to stay out of it," Despoina pouted. "I wanted to see what it was like to bond with you."

Rhyslin chuckled. "It might be better that you weren't there. They stripped her bare and presented her to me in the baths. I thought that she might crawl into the cold pool and hide." He shook his head. "But she didn't. She offered all of herself to me and was happy she gave only herself."

The diviner flashed a rare smile, having grown used to not being able to see Rhyslin. "I will consider it a boon if you'd watch over her. She'd be one if I were the kind to take Taghta."

"As if I had a choice," Rhyslin groused, making Ananke laugh. "A Mathair has seen fit to bring headstrong women into my life."

Ananke gazed at him. "Is that good or bad?"

Rhyslin shrugged. "Good, I think. They'll keep me on my feet."

"And in your bed," Rana quipped, blushing as she teased Rhyslin. "I've never seen Momma happier than she is now."

"That is nice to hear," Ananke smiled at Rana. Mathair Astinmah wanted Flur and Ria to be happy and cared for, and he also worked hard to find women who would make Rhyslin happy."

"Mathair and I might occasionally disagree on things, but she has always wanted what's best for her children," Rhyslin commented as he leaned back in his chair. "I spent too many years fighting against what is the best thing in my life."

"We never know how things will turn out until we are hit in the face with them," Despoina said, smiling ruefully. "Will you come again and visit us? I promise not to be afraid."

Rhyslin nodded. "It would be my honor." He flashed her a playful grin. "Are you trying to get rid of us?"

"No, not at all," Despoina sputtered in surprise. "We just figured you had something important to get back and do."

"Not at all," Rhyslin guaranteed her. "Things at home will keep for a while. It's not every day that I get to spend some time with beautiful goddesses."

"Not every day," Rana snickered, "Just once or twice a month."

"Hush you," Rhyslin wagged a finger at the young spell-blade. "If you don't behave, I'll spank you again."

"Yes, Maighstir," Rana blushed, garnering good-natured laughter from the two goddesses. Rather than feel offended by the laughter, Rana accepted it as laughter between friends.

Rhyslin spent the next several hours deep in conversation with the two diathan, and Rana spent that time trying to stay awake, finally giving up and resting her head on the table.

"I think we wore her out," Ananke whispered as they finished up and noticed that the young spell blade was asleep.

Rhyslin smiled as he brushed his fingers through Rana's hair, drawing a soft moan from her. "So it seems."

"Can we help you?" Despoina inquired as she gazed at Rana.

"If you can open a doorway back to the manse, I can get her," Rhyslin commented as he scooped Rana up and settled his staff across her body.

With a nod, Ananke created a doorway and whispered. "We will see you again, Mac Draoidheachd. Please don't be a stranger."

"I'll do my best, and thank you for the tea and cookies." He replied as he stepped through the doorway.

Chapter Fourteen
The Bonds of Hearth and Heart

After stepping through the portal, Rhyslin cradled the sleeping Rana closer to his chest and slowly ascended the stairs to the mansion's front door. If he was surprised to find Flur waiting for him, it didn't show. "Thank you, Flur. Are Ria and Rowena still awake?"

Flur shook her head. "Rowena went to sleep earlier after finding out where you disappeared. Ria is still awake and is somewhat concerned about Rana."

Rhyslin nodded. "Would you grab the staff and take it to the study, then find Ria and meet me there." When Flur smiled and nodded, he started up the stairs. "I'm going to put this little one to bed."

The blonde-haired bhanna kissed Rhyslin on the cheek as she reached up to take his staff. "We'll meet you there," she said. Then she turned in place, her skirt rising to show off her thighs, and danced down the hallway.

Rhyslin watched her, sucking in a slow, appreciative breath, then with a slight shake of his head, he made his way down the hallway to Rana's room and deposited her on the bed. "Sweet Dreams, mo phrìseil," he whispered as he kissed her cheek. The young Hin I-Balanath mumbled something under her breath as she settled deeper into sleep.

After tucking her in, Rhyslin carefully shut the door behind him and went to the study on the second floor, near the library. He paused just outside, listening as Ria asked, "Did he say anything?"

"No, just to meet him here," Flur's whispered voice replied.

Listening to Ria, Rhyslin came to the realization that she was a good mother, one who was always worried about her daughter. "I guess I should call her our daughter now." Rhyslin briefly considered before walking through the door. "Ladies, I hope we didn't scare you too badly."

He had a second to set himself before both women burrowed under his arms and hugged him. "Welcome home, Maighstir," Flur whispered against the soft skin of his throat.

"You did give us a start. At least you did until Rowena told us where you were." Ria murmured as she nuzzled his chest. "What did Ananke and Despoina want?"

Rhyslin led them over to the couch and sat down, then waited while they made themselves comfortable against him.

"Where do I start?" He paused to gather his thoughts. "Ananke was acting as hostess for Despoina so that she would have someone she could see and interact with."

Ria looked up, her nose wrinkled in confusion. "I don't understand. Is Despoina Blind?"

Rhyslin shook his head. "Only where I'm concerned. Her divination is so integral to her life that she has difficulty talking to a person without a destiny."

Flur blinked. "You don't have a destiny?" She had never heard of such a thing. "How is that possible?"

"It beats me," Rhyslin shrugged. I don't for some reason, which is odd. She says she can interact with the Diathan, so they have a limited destiny."

"Hmmm," Flur hummed. "So, Ananke was there so that Despoina could see you?"

"I guess." Rhyslin wasn't sure about that, but let it drop for now. "I think it was more that she couldn't use her divination on me, and it made her uncomfortable."

"That makes sense," Flur reasoned as she cuddled closer to him. "So what did she say about Rana?"

"I've changed her destiny and continue to do so with each day she's here." He still didn't understand why that was a problem, because the way he saw it, each new day brought changes with it.

Ria raised her head. "Is the change for the better or the worse?" She bit her lips as she tried to hide her fearful concern.

Rhyslin looked down into Ria's eyes, "Before I answer that, I want you to listen carefully and let me finish." When she nodded, he brushed a kiss against her forehead.

"Okay. Despoina has been following Rana's destiny since birth. She saved a group of people in her original destiny but died doing it."

Other than a soft gasp, Ria didn't make a sound. "Now that she's met me, her destiny has changed. She saves that same group of people but gets seriously injured doing it." He watched Ria, nodding as she remained calm.

"She can't see any further because Rana's destiny changes daily. If I get her more training in draoidheachd, swordsmanship, and survival, she'll survive her destiny with nary a lasting wound."

"Thank you, Mathair," Ria breathed as she tried to get closer to Rhyslin. "What are your plans for Rana?"

"I'm going to have Rembran further her training while teaching her more about the different spheres of draoidheachd."

285

When Ria nodded, Rhyslin leaned his head back against the top of the couch cushions. "I'm also going to ask Marcus to train her in survival skills."

A stifled yawn brought his attention to where Flur was almost asleep, curled against him.

"Thank you, Maighstir," Ria murmured as she rested her head on his chest. "For taking care of my daughter and me." She mumbled as she closed her eyes and listened to the sound of his heartbeat. When her breathing evened out, he looked down to find her asleep. He was thankful that the couch was comfortable. Before he knew it, he closed his eyes and joined the two women in slumber.

"Well, if you three don't look comfy."

Rhyslin slowly awoke to find Rowena standing there with her hands on her hips. He could tell she wasn't mad even though she was tapping her foot.

"We didn't intend on sleeping here. It just sort of happened." Rhyslin shrugged. "We were talking about Rana and ended up falling asleep."

Rowena smiled as she leaned down and kissed him. "I know. Despoina told me about what happened last night." She tenderly brushed her fingers through his hair. "Are you hungry?"

While Rhyslin was thinking about it, Ria mumbled. "Yes, I was so worried that I didn't eat last night."

Flur rubbed the sleep out of her eyes and gazed up at Rowena. "I'll get breakfast started as soon as I get up."

The Seeress waved her off. "Why don't you three get cleaned up? I'll take care of getting breakfast ready." She leaned in and hugged Ria and Flur.

Rhyslin looked at Ria and Flur, who nodded. "That sounds good to me." He pushed off the couch, stretched, and waited for the two Bannaichean to join him before heading to the baths.

On the way, they stopped by Rana's room to awaken her.

A half-hour later, feeling much more awake, they went to the kitchen and joined Rowena for breakfast.

"What are your plans for today?" Rowena asked as the four took their places at the table. While she waited for Rhyslin to answer, she served breakfast to Ria, Flur, and Rana.

The draoidh took a bite out of his bread. "I need to talk with Rembran and see if he'll train Rana," he said.

"Hey, I don't need training," the young spell-blade complained.

Rhyslin cut her off, "Yes, you do. What you know might be enough to beat a non-spell-blade, but you'd never be able to beat Rembran in one-on-one combat. He may be an apprentice pilot, but he's one of the best spell-blades in the army."

When Rana gave him a dubious look, he waggled his finger at her. "He's beaten me more often than I've beaten him." He dropped his hand to tap the tabletop. "He may not look it, but he's almost as good as Marcus, and Marcus isn't a spell blade." He attempted to impart wisdom. "You couldn't ask for a better teacher than him."

"He's better than you?" Rana couldn't believe he had admitted that to her.

289

"Yes, I'm not a spell-blade. I might be able to beat him using pure draoidheacd, but he can use that sword and shield to a greater advantage. He can wear me out and take me down before I can take his weapons away from him."

"Can you use a sword?" Rana inquired, not ready to believe him completely.

"Yes, but not nearly as well as Rembran or Marcus can. All Soldiers must be familiar with swords and knives, but people like me aren't required to specialize."

"I didn't know that," Rana commented, a thoughtful look on her face.

Rhyslin nodded as another thought crossed his mind. "I might ask Marcus to train you in basic wilderness survival."

Rana's eyes lit up. "Really?" When he nodded again, she smiled broadly. "I'd love to learn that."

"Will you watch the training?" Rana inquired excitedly.

"I think not," Rhyslin looked at her. "While you are working with him, I will talk to Andros and Ixa." Rhyslin didn't want to get into a discussion about the crystal. "About re-negotiating their contract."

"Oh, okay." The young spell-blade mumbled as she took a bite of her food.

Rhyslin and his group were halfway finished with breakfast before Rembran and his two companions appeared.

"Good morning, sir." Rembran greeted as he eyed the remains of the meal before reaching out. He paused, looking to Rhyslin for permission.

"By all means," Rhyslin pointed at the empty chairs on the table's far side. "Eat up. You're going to be busy."

"Doing what?" Ixa inquired as she sat down beside her maighstir and grabbed a biscuit. She smiled as she cut the biscuit and dabbed on some jelly.

Rhyslin pointed at Rana, "Training her."

The older spellblade took a bite of his biscuit as he gazed at the young woman. "Hmm. How good is she?" He wasn't asking about her because he was doubtful. He was asking one military person for his opinion on a recruit.

"She beat me to a standstill on the courthouse stairs." Rhyslin finished his biscuit and reached for another. "Or she would have if we were fighting for real. She's got basic training, Rembran. She needs advanced training, and you're one of the best Spell-blades I know."

Rembran finished the biscuit and wiped his mouth. "Okay. When do we start?"

"Now." Rhyslin grinned.

"For how long a day?"

Rhyslin thought it over. "Four hours a day before I get her for three hours." He was planning her training schedule. "Then Marcus will work with her for a couple of hours."

Rembran nodded, "So, she'll have ten hours a day of training." He paused, considering something. "How about we break up her scheduling? I get her four hours every other day, you get her three hours a day, and Marcus gets her four hours on the days I don't train her."

The draoidh tapped his finger on the tabletop. "That would work better." He looked at Rana and asked, "Can you keep up a schedule like that?"

It was her turn to think it over. She wondered if she could keep up with such a busy schedule. She almost refused but knew that she had to at least try.

She lowered her head, cradling it in her hand, wishing that she could just be a normal woman who didn't have to worry about the future. She hurriedly wiped away her tears before Rhyslin saw them. She didn't think he would understand why she was upset. She covertly wiped the tears again, wishing that she could be happy, if only for a little while.

Unknown to her, both men heard her quiet sobs. Rembran arched a brow in her direction.

Rhyslin nodded as he put an arm around her. "I know. It hurts, doesn't it? If all of this disappeared, you could have a normal life."

Rana looked up at him, anguish on her face. "But I can't, can I?" She desperately wanted him to say she could.

"You can. Nobody is forcing you to do anything." He pulled her and her chair closer. "Your life is up to you."

"What about Despoina's prophecy? What will happen to those people if I don't do what I'm supposed to do?"

Rhyslin silently cursed the prophecy. More than anything, he wanted Rana to live free and be happy. "What's going to happen to people in the future will happen whether or not you are there." He paused.

"The only thing that will be different is how many will die." He closed his eyes as he attempted to peer into the future. "I'm not Despoina, and I can't give you a guarantee." He reached out to caress her cheek. "The best you can do is be who you are. Nobody can ask for more."

Rana collapsed against him, sobbing as she wondered what he'd think about her if she walked away from her destiny.

"No matter what you decide, I will love you, for you. That will never change."

Rhyslin held her as best as possible, giving her the needed support.

The young spell-blade clung to him until her crisis was over, then slowly pushed herself up and looked into Rhysln's eyes. "I can do it." She shook her head. "I will do it."

Rhyslin nodded once. "Just do your best. Nobody can ask for more." He leaned back in his chair, crossing his arms over his chest. He gave them time to finish their breakfast, and when Rembran pushed away from the table, Ixa started to do the same.

"Ixa, would you and Andros stay for a few mionaidean? I need to talk to both of you."

"Of course, Maighstir Darkblade," Ixa replied after glancing at Andros. She settled back into the chair and watched as Rembran led Rana outside.

Once Rhyslin and the two elementals were alone, he leaned forward. "Do you need the crystal to stay on this plane?"

Caught by surprise, Andros sucked in a breath. "Well, no. We can stay on this plane indefinitely."

Ixa nodded. "That's right. We only need it as a reference point to control the ship and what's in it." She quirked an eyebrow. "Why?"

"Because I've been thinking of releasing you from the crystal and paying you for your work," Rhyslin stated.

Silence reigned as the two elementals listened to him. Ixa glanced at Andros and caught the skeptical look in his eyes. "May I ask why?"

Rhyslin blew out a slow breath. "If you hadn't been bound to the crystal, Meron would have never been able to hurt you. Because you were bound to the crystal, he had a weak spot to exploit." He waved his hand in dismissal of the recently stilled mage. "You deserve better."

Ixa was excited, as she wanted to remain bound to Rembran. She didn't need any payment, as she enjoyed what she did, but the money could be useful to Rembran. "When can we do it, break from the Crystal?"

Andros tapped his toes. "It sounds good, and while you are at it, you can pull all that copper wire from the ship's frame. We don't need it." He grinned. "You'd have either more cargo space or more crew space."

Rhyslin stroked his chin, "Very well." He drew a sigil in the air, summoning the crystal into his hands. "Once we pull all the copper out, you can use that room for your quarters." Looking at the two, he placed the crystal on the tabletop and gestured, "Go ahead, destroy it."

He watched as Ixa and Andros rendered the crystal into reddish dust.

"Now that it's done, I have another question." When Ixa blinked, he continued, "Do you know of any other elementals who would want to work for the Soarca or me?"

The air elemental licked her lips as she thought it over. "I might know of a few air elementals that want to leave Tuiteam gaoithe." She shrugged, "I'd have to ask around."

"I don't have to ask," Andros said. I know at least eight earth elementals that want out of Taigh na Cloiche."

The two iron elementals working the dockyard were evidence of that.

"If you can, I need four air and earth elementals who don't mind working together," Rhyslin commented. "Maybe more if I build more ships and skiffs."

"That shouldn't be a problem," Ixa grinned. "I can find you four maighdeannan if Andros can find four fir, and they'll get along as well as Andros, and I do." She wondered how to tell him that there were very few males on her home plane, and all the women she knew wanted to meet men.

Andros quirked a brow as he listened to Ixa. If she weren't going to tell Rhyslin, he wouldn't either. The elemental world was a study of balances. Just as her world was one of women, his was one of men. That was why opposite elemental beings got along well.

Rhyslin watched them for a few mionaidean, waiting for one of them to explain. When they didn't, he shrugged. "How long will it take you to contact your friends?" The draoidh inquired.

The corners of Ixa's mouth curled up. "Not long if we can borrow a communications crystal."

Andros blinked, wondering what game Ixa was playing. As elementals, they didn't need to use crystals. When he realized she was teasing Rhyslin, he hid his own smile.

"Hmmmph," Rhyslin groused, catching onto her joke. "Next, I suppose you'll want me to pay the toll?"

Ixa froze, examining his face. For a moment, she was afraid she'd screwed up. She cringed and started to apologize until she saw the faint signs of amusement.

"You're mean, Maighstir Rhyslin. You had me thinking you were mad at me."

301

The draoidh shrugged, "I've heard that from Rana." He chuckled, "Sometimes she thinks I'm the dark one himself." He offered a half bow to the two. "You are, at this moment, freed from our contract." He watched Ixa's face transform into rapturous joy. "I guess you'll be bonding with Rembran."

The air elemental nodded happily. "I will." She gave Rhyslin an imploring look. "May I please go to him?"

"Fine, fine." He laughed. "Go to your Maighstir, tell him the good news. We'll discuss your new contracts later."

Without waiting for him to finish, Ixa ran down the hallway.

Chapter Fifteen
The Web and the Mirror

Despite its name, the residents of Long Sleep never truly rested. The necropolis pulsed with a kind of unlife, slow, deliberate, unending. Between crumbling archways and bone-strewn avenues, Skellet-zauberer — liches — lingered over ancient tomes, their fingers of polished ivory tracing runes that still smoked with blue fire. Skelletkrieger — ancient skeletal warriors, marched in endless drills, armor clattering like distant hail. Wiedergänger — unliving corpses, shambled through the dust, their half-decayed forms serving the will of master's they could no longer name.

The air was thick with the scent of dry rot and ozone.

Pale motes drifted through the stillness like ash, catching what little light the black sun offered, a bruised and dying glow that never warmed the skin. Beneath it, Meron and his bonds had settled into this city of bones, making a temporary home among ruins that whispered in the wind.

Only three beings took no part in the restless labor: Macraww, the unliving guardian, sat perched atop the tallest column, a figure carved from death itself, watching over the endless necropolis with the patience of stone.

Death lay curled at the base of that same column, vast and still, its ribcage rising and falling with the slow rhythm of a world long since dead. Against those ribs leaned Despair, helm bowed, the faint blue fire beneath it flickering low.

It had been three days since they arrived in Long Sleep. In that strange half-light, the days bled together, time had no pulse here. It was the first time since Despair's arrival on Crann Na Beatha that he felt untouched by the gaze of the Nan Diathan. Even the tug of the great wheel, that inexorable pull of divine design, was muted, distant, as if the world itself had drawn a breath and held it.

{What do you think of Meronkae and his bonds?} The rumbling voice of Death reverberated through Despair's mind, deep as the grinding of mountains.

The flames under his helmet flared briefly at the name of the renegade magus, the one who had betrayed his friends to follow the spider god.

{Meron is almost fanatically driven,} Despair replied, his tone measured but edged.

It was to be expected of those who served the spider-god. {His bonds act like the ancient maenads. They will do whatever Meron tells them to do.}

{He is gathering interesting followers this time around,} the skelletdrache observed. {A half-drake, a fanatical magus, fearless bonds, a witch-priestess.} He turned his skull toward the black sun, its light reflected in the hollow of his eyes. {And this army of the unliving. What do you think his plans will be?}

The Todesritter didn't answer. Wind passed through the bone columns with a low, mournful hum, like the sigh of a world that had forgotten how to live.

Despair only watched the black sun shimmer faintly in the horizon's pall. He had no answer, only the memory of a god who had been locked away for millennia.

Meron held the cracked mirror in his hand, fingers curled around the delicate silver frame. The glass was cold, its fractured surface reflecting shards of candlelight that splintered his face into a dozen distorted versions of himself. Dust drifted lazily through the stale air of the crypt, catching in the dim glow that leaked through a fissure in the ceiling. Somewhere deeper in the tomb, the slow drip of water echoed, marking time with the patience of centuries.

His eyes followed the fractures across the mirror as though tracing veins beneath skin, trying to divine the wellbeing of his soldiers through the web of cracks.

Other than an occasional twitch, he betrayed no emotion.

{This mirror is too small; I need something bigger.} He projected the thought to his fair-haired bond.

His gaze was distant, fixed beyond the walls of the crypt, as though he could already see the shape of what he desired forming in the darkness beyond.

The fair-haired woman inclined her head, the faint shimmer of candlelight catching in her hair. {I have counted no less than six skellet-zauberer. Might one them be able to help you?}

The fabric of Meron's robe whispered softly as he reached out, the touch of his gloved hand brushing against hers. {As always, you give me options I had not considered.}

He could feel her pride surge through the bond, a living pulse beneath the weight of stone and dust, and he leaned down, stealing a kiss from her. The faint scent of myrrh and cold metal lingered in the air between them. {I will return shortly.}

If his acknowledgment had brightened her world, his act of affection was nothing short of an emotional starburst, a radiant, intoxicating burst that drowned out all reason. In that moment, her devotion to her master deepened, blooming like a flower in the dark.

As he crossed the threshold of the crypt, Meron's boots stirred a thin veil of ash that had settled over the ancient stone. The air beyond was cold and heavy, tasting faintly of metal and dust. His eyes adjusted quickly to the unnatural darkness of Long Sleep, where even shadows seemed to breathe.

Above, through cracks in the cavern's ceiling, the black sun flickered faintly, its light bleeding through in muted pulses that glimmered against the marble bones of forgotten temples. For a moment, beneath that strange imitation of daylight, he forgot that he was deep underground.

As always, the gifts from the spider god reminded him of his status as a favored servant. A faint hum ran beneath his skin where the divine sigils rested, a soft vibration like the echo of a distant heartbeat.

He started toward the nearest dark cathedral, the sound of his footsteps swallowed by the stillness that ruled this place. Towering columns of calcified bone lined the main thoroughfare, each carved with the runes of the dead. From their hollow eyes, faint motes of ghostlight drifted like fireflies.

As he passed beneath them, the vast guardian perched on the central spire tilted his skull-like head, the motion creaking faintly. The creature's empty sockets followed Meron's path, and though it wondered briefly at his purpose, it did not stir.

Meron's faith in the spider god deterred the few Wiedergänger and Skelettkrieger he encountered. The zombies shrank back into the alcoves of ruined shrines, while the skeletal warriors froze mid-step, weapons lowered in mute acknowledgment of his divine favor. He did not spare them a glance as he continued toward the dwelling of the unliving magi.

Not many minutes later, Meron stood before what, on the surface, might once have been a grand cathedral. Its facade loomed from the gloom like a fossilized mountain, its spires broken but still defiant against the subterranean vault. The stained glass panels that formed its windows shimmered faintly under the black light, casting fractured hues of violet and green across the cracked flagstones.

Unlike the scenes of the Nan Diathan, these panes depicted the rise and fall of chaos, and, in twisting mosaics of bone-white and crimson, the events that had transformed a once-living magus into a Skellet-zauberer.

The light that passed through them did not bless, but blighted, painting Meron's face in the colors of devotion, ruin, and divine corruption.

Schooling his expression into one of quiet discipline, Meron approached the solid iron door. The surface was cold and pitted with age, its black sheen broken by etchings that glowed faintly like veins of molten silver. He placed his right hand upon the center square and waited patiently to be recognized. The metal thrummed beneath his palm, not with heat, but with awareness, as if the door itself were drawing breath in anticipation.

{You may enter, Magus Meron, servant of the spider god, Iktomi.} The mental voice of the unliving mage echoed in his mind, hollow and toneless, yet carrying the weight of ancient authority.

At the invitation, the door shuddered and creaked open, its hinges grinding in protest after centuries of disuse. A stale breath of air rolled out, thick with the scent of candle soot and old parchment.

What had once been a space of worship now resembled a scholar's tomb, shelves bowed beneath draoidheil tomes, black candles guttered in the stillness, and glass instruments glowed faintly with necromantic light. Wisps of dust swirled lazily in the gloom, disturbed only by Meron's deliberate steps.

He wisely kept his hands to himself as he made his way through the cluttered chamber, the sound of his boots muffled against rugs long stiff with age. Strange sigils pulsed faintly on the walls, reacting to his presence, but he ignored their whispering shimmer. Somewhere deeper within, the faint hum of power, like distant insects beneath stone, marked the dwelling of the unliving wizard he sought.

He finally found the skellet-zauberer in what once might have been the cathedral's apse. Broken stained glass framed the alcove, its fractured panes still catching light from the guttering candles, throwing shards of color over the lich's pale bones. The creature sat motionless before what had once been an altar, its spine curved like a question mark of defiance against eternity.

The lich turned its head slowly, the motion deliberate and creaking, as if the air itself resisted the movement of its ancient bones. Its unliving eyes fixed upon its guest, the green fires within burning with a steady, baleful light. That ghostly glow flickered against the polished iron of an empty suit of armor that stood sentinel nearby, throwing distorted reflections across the chamber's stone walls. The air was dry and cold, saturated with the faint scent of old ashes and something metallic, as though the very air remembered blood.

{What is it you seek, Magus Meron?}

"I have men that are on the move, and this—" he withdrew the fractured mirror from his robe and offered it to the lich to examine, "while serving its purpose, cannot show me where they are."

Meron's voice echoed faintly in the quiet of the lich's laboratory, absorbed by shelves of bottled shadows and rune-etched glass.

The Skellet-zauberer took the mirror in bony fingers that clicked faintly against the silvered surface, careful as a jeweler handling something fragile. {It is an elegant communication object, but it's not designed to see much. A clear pool of water would do better.}

Meron was disciplined enough not to roll his eyes, though he felt the familiar prick of irritation rise like heat under his skin. "You are correct, and if I had a pool of water, I would use it."

The lich handed him back the mirror with a sound like parchment brushing against stone. {I can help you with your scrying problem.}

The Skellet-zauberer inclined its head, the vertebrae along its neck shifting like grinding clockwork, and gestured toward a massive onyx table in the center of the chamber. Its surface was carved with delicate channels filled with faintly glowing dust, a living map of the world above. {Please place your mirror here,} it said, indicating the edge of the stone.

Meron approached, boots scraping softly against the obsidian floor. A thin chill crept through the soles of his shoes. He placed the mirror on the indicated corner and raised a brow, studying the interplay of dark stone and reflected green fire.

{Think about who you want to see and their current position will glow on the table.} The Skellet-zauberer's tone was as smooth and cold as the mineral before them.

Fighting the urge to curse the lich, Meron exhaled through his nose, slow and measured. He closed his eyes and conjured the captain's face in his mind, the scar at his chin, the set of his jaw. He had hoped to speak with his men, to hear their voices through the mirror's glass, but their position alone would have to suffice.

When he opened his eyes, a faint light stirred on the map's surface, a glow like frost forming in moonlight. It brightened, resolving into a cluster of marks near the northern curve of the River Sten. Meron leaned closer, his breath fogging faintly in the cold air.

All twenty-five soldiers were standing on the banks, a mere thirty-three leagues from Oak Grove. Unless they borrowed several boats, it would take them weeks to leave the Saorsa and reach the mountains.

He straightened, the brief flare of hope cooling to resignation. "You have my thanks for your assistance." He gave a half bow, retrieving the fractured mirror and tucking it carefully into his robe. The glass felt colder now, heavier, as if it had absorbed the lich's presence.

The lich did not reply. It watched him in silence, eyes burning with patient, unblinking light as the living magus turned and made his way toward the cavern's archway. Behind him, the faint hum of the onyx table subsided, and only the whisper of distant dripping water disturbed the stillness of the dead.

Meron waited until the last trace of the Skellet-Zauberer's presence faded from his senses, that faint, metallic hum that seemed to cling to the bones of the cavern.

Only when the air felt still again did he stop, turning toward the dim blue shimmer of the exit. The chill of the underworld clung to his robe, the scent of dust and withered incense thick in his lungs.

He drew the fractured mirror from his sleeve and, with deliberate care, closed his fingers around it. The glass was cold, heavy, almost resentful of his touch.

He bowed his head and whispered, "Great Weaver, whose web strides the sky. Please cleanse the unliving taint from this, your instrument of divine gaze."

The air grew taut, humming faintly as though invisible threads were being plucked all around him.

Under his fingers, the mirror warmed, first to body temperature, then hotter, until it nearly burned his palm. Then, with a sigh like wind through silk, it cooled again.

A voice drifted from the mirror, smooth and sibilant, echoing faintly in his mind: {Your men are working out their latest problem.}

The words slithered through the air, intimate and dry. The spider god didn't sound offended.

Meron's lips twitched in a faint, private smile. He shrugged, ready to move on, but the warmth beneath his fingers flared again. {I need you to perform a task for me, Meronkae.}

He froze. A sudden pressure, light as silk, sharp as claws, brushed his scalp. The touch sank through skin and thought alike, and he shivered as though shadowed legs had crept across his mind.

{What is your will, my lord?}

The cavern filled with a susurrus of whispering threads, too soft to be called words.

Meron listened, eyes unfocused, while the god's command coiled through him. Each phrase seemed to pull another thread tight, mentions of his home-plane, of servants long forsaken, of a path to spread chaos and discord like a creeping web.

By the time the voice faded, Meron's pulse had quickened. The divine chill receded, leaving him flushed and restless. {I will deliver your words, my Master.}

His voice trembled with barely contained eagerness. He pressed the mirror to his chest, reverently, then turned and strode toward the light ahead. The echo of his boots faded into the stillness, and somewhere behind him, unseen, the faint glimmer of a web lingered in the air before vanishing into dust.

He could barely hide his excitement as he hurried off to deliver Death and Despair their orders.

Chapter Sixteen
The Spellblade's Trial & the Smith's Gift

The morning mist still clung to the practice field, curling low around the worn edges of the sparring circles. Dew silvered the grass, and the faint tang of steel and sweat drifted in the cool air, a familiar scent of training, determination, and old bruises. The rhythmic clang of distant blades rang out from another corner of the grounds, but here, the world seemed to hold its breath.

Rana stood near the center, the toes of her boots pressed into the damp soil. Her hazel eyes were fixed on the man before her, and her right hand rested lightly on the hilt of her sword, not tense, but ready.

The faintest ripple of wind caught her loose hair and brushed it against her cheek, a reminder of how exposed she felt under her instructor's scrutiny.

Rembran stood opposite, the bottom edge of his kite shield resting in the earth. He leaned casually against it, his stance deceptively relaxed. Behind the ease, there was weight, the quiet confidence of a man who had fought real battles. He studied the young Hin I-Balanath before him, his eyes sharp beneath the weathered lines at their corners.

He nodded once at her footing, his expression approving. With an inward smile, he spoke, his voice carrying across the field like gravel smoothed by years of discipline.

"Before we begin the testing, I want to ask a few questions."

Hearing that, Rana allowed a slow breath to escape, the tension easing from her shoulders. The cool air stung pleasantly in her lungs.

"Okay. What would you like to know?"

She was watching Rembran as closely as he was watching her. Though his weight leaned idly on the shield, she could sense the coiled readiness in him, the way a hawk might seem still until the instant it strikes.

"Which would you rather be called, Vuuroena or Rana?"

The question caught her off guard. For a heartbeat, the sounds of the field fell away, the distant shouts, the clatter of practice swords, the wind through the poplar trees that lined the yard. Her thoughts flickered briefly to Rhyslin.

"Rana will be fine, Maighstir Rembran." After all, it's what Rhyslin called her, and she was comfortable with it.

Rembran inclined his head. "Then Rana it is."

He took a moment to look her over, not unkindly, the measured gaze of a soldier taking stock.

Her skirt fell in practical folds to her knees, the slits allowing movement. Her blouse was thick-weave cotton, stiffened just enough to offer some protection; her boots, solid leather to the knee, had been well-oiled and well-worn. Even the way her hair was tied, loose enough to fall free, tight enough not to distract, spoke of readiness.

He nodded slightly to himself. "Do you mind if I ask who trained you?"

Rana's mouth curved into a quick grin, sunlight catching the faint flush in her cheeks. "Eriand Silver-blade trained me."

She said it with pride, not arrogance, but respect, and there was a shimmer of memory in her tone: long afternoons of drills, her master's calm voice correcting her stance. She knew Eriand's name carried weight among her people, a title almost mythic.

Rembran's brow lifted faintly in recognition. "I've heard of him," he acknowledged. "Rhyslin says that he's the Captain of the Guard for your people's council." His eyes dropped briefly to the single blade at her hip. "Do you use just one blade or dual-wield?"

Rana's brow furrowed, her thumb tracing the curve of the sword hilt. "Maighstir Eriand only uses one blade, so he taught me that."

She wet her lips, a small, human gesture in a ritual moment. "I've considered learning to use an arming sword or dagger but have never found anyone to teach me." She met his eyes with the quiet directness of one issuing a challenge. "Can you teach me?"

Rembran's lips curved in a slow, knowing smile. "I might know someone who can teach you," he admitted.

"I, myself, use a sword and shield. So, I could teach you that style of fighting."

Rana tilted her head, considering, her eyes flicking from his weapon to the scars etched faintly in his armor. The air between them seemed to tighten, humming with unspoken curiosity.

"That could be helpful during a field fight," she said after a moment, "but I don't know if I'll ever be in one."

Again, Rembran nodded, his shield shifting slightly as he straightened. "I can work with that."

He gave her a heartbeat's pause, a soldier's courtesy before engagement, then hefted his shield into position. The leather straps creaked softly as he slid his arm through, the movement smooth and sure. The stillness of the field thickened, every sound seeming distant.

"Let's see what you can do."

The words fell like a spark into dry tinder.

The moment Rembran spoke, *"Let's see what you can do,"* the world seemed to narrow around Rana.

Blood pulsed in her ears, a steady drum beneath the quiet murmur of onlookers. She felt her pulse echo down her sword arm.

Her hand dropped to the hilt, the familiar weight of the weapon grounding her. Beneath her boots, the soil was firm but slick with morning dew, and she shifted her left leg back to find her balance.

With a slow, deliberate breath, she drew the blade. Steel whispered against the sheath. a sound like a sigh cutting through the still air. The sword caught the light as it rose, and she brought it level with her shoulder, steady, graceful, a stance her master would have approved of.

Even though her thoughts raced a mile a minute, she moved as if through calm water. Her heart thundered; her body obeyed. A faint smile curved her lips as she remembered what Rhyslin had done in their duel.

"*Apprehendens umbram,*" she whispered.

The words carried power, the syllables curling into the air like smoke. The shadows at Rembran's back quivered, thickened, and surged upward into the shape of a spectral hand. Its fingers of living darkness coiled around his ankle and held fast. The air around the field cooled sharply, the sunlight dimming as though the world held its breath. Rana's sword lanced out in *splitting the sheave*, its arc clean and bright against the gloom.

Feeling the tug around his ankle, Rembran's grin flashed, not surprise, but delight. He tapped his foot sharply against the ground, the heel scraping a faint rune into the dirt. Light bled through the lines, a soft gold that burst upward in a sudden flare. The brilliance cut through the shadow's grip like sunlight through mist. The air snapped, the spell dissipated, and the cold receded.

His grin turned feral. He shifted his stance, armor creaking faintly, and threw his weight behind his shield. Rana's thrust met its curve with a sharp *clang*, sparks spitting from the contact. He pushed, twisting his sword in a wide arc, expecting to catch her in the counter.

But she was already gone.

Rana spun to the left, her boots whispering over the grass, and brought her blade back to her center in a single, fluid motion.

Her skirt flared with the turn, and her braid snapped like a dark ribbon behind her.

Rembran advanced again, fast and precise. The shield came up in a heavy sweep, an attempt to corner her with brute force.

Rana saw the motion coming, the quick shift of his shoulder, the faint hiss of air as the shield carved its path, and stepped aside just in time. The rush of wind from the swing brushed her sleeve.

He dragged the shield to the right, barely intercepting her sideways slash. The impact rang hollow, steel against wood and iron. Rana gave a curt nod — acknowledging the deflection, and slid her sword along the rim of the shield in a grating slide that sent shivers down the blade.

As he passed her, she ducked low, pivoted, and planted her heel behind his knee.

The impact was solid, a dull *thump* of boot meeting armor. She thought, fleetingly, that Maighstir Eriand would frown at such a maneuver. Then she smirked.

Rembran's knee buckled slightly. In the space of a heartbeat, he made his choice: hold the shield and crash, or let go and move. He released it.

The great kite shield hit the ground with a heavy *thud* as he rolled forward, shoulder-first, the dirt streaking his armor. He came up smoothly, his sword sweeping back in a defensive arc over his shoulder, a motion so practiced it looked effortless. When his blade met no resistance, he blinked, turned, and found Rana standing on his shield.

The raven-haired woman grinned down at him, daring, triumphant, the sunlight glinting off her blade.

Rembran barked a laugh. Inspiration struck when he caught sight of Ixa and Andros standing at the edge of the field, watching with rapt attention.

[*Andros, can you push my shield up from the ground?*]

At his mental command, the earth elemental nodded once. Rembran's fingers traced a sigil in the air, golden dust sparking where his fingertip passed.

Rana frowned, her brow creasing as she tried to interpret the glowing mark. The symbol shimmered, twisting, and then the ground answered.

The shield exploded upward beneath her feet.

A rush of displaced air struck her face. She dropped to one knee, her hand slapping down to steady herself as the shield tipped, teetered, then slewed sideways.

With a startled cry, she lost balance entirely. The world tilted.

She hit the ground hard enough to knock the breath from her lungs, and her sword spun from her grasp, flashing once before tumbling into the crowd.

For a heartbeat, the only sound was the ringing echo of steel landing somewhere among the watchers. Dust rose around her in a soft golden haze.

Knowing she wouldn't get help from the peanut gallery, Rana gritted her teeth, reached into her left boot, and drew her dagger. The smaller blade gleamed dully in the sunlight, wicked and sure.

When Rembran approached, cautious, curious, she hunched, faking a limp. Her voice came thin and pained, a convincing little whimper.

Rembran slowed, watching her rock on one leg. He couldn't tell whether she was acting or truly hurt. The crowd murmured, tension building like a held breath.

He was so focused on her supposed injury that he almost missed the shift in her weight, the twitch of her shoulder, the coil of her muscles. She lunged, fast as a viper, driving for his foot.

"I don't think so," he muttered.

His sword fell from his hand as he caught her wrist mid-thrust. The impact jarred up both their arms. He twisted, using his strength to wrench her arm behind her back. She gasped as he forced her to her knees, the dirt cold beneath them.

Before she could react, he stripped the dagger from her hand and pressed its own keen edge to her throat.

"Yield."

The blade's chill kissed her skin. Rana froze, her chest heaving. The faintest bead of sweat ran down her temple.

Feeling the keenness of her blade pressed to her throat, she gasped, "I yield."

"Thank goodness," he breathed, releasing her. His voice carried the warmth of relief, not triumph. "You'd make Eriand proud."

When she turned on one knee and raised her hand for her dagger, he handed it back, hilt-first, with a small nod of respect. He stepped back as she sheathed it carefully in her boot. The murmur of the crowd swelled again, approval, admiration, a few good-natured laughs.

The duel was over, but something between them had changed.

She had earned his respect, not by victory, but by courage, cunning, and refusal to yield until forced to.

Rana looked up at him, her breath still quick from the fight, considering his words. The tension in her shoulders slowly eased as the adrenaline began to fade. Around them, the murmur of the practice field returned, clinking weapons, low voices, the rhythmic thud of training dummies being struck. She gave a short, decisive nod.

"I keep finding some things that you and Maighstir Rhyslin do unfair, but I've grown to understand that there is no fairness in combat. There's just living and dying."

She straightened, brushed dust from her knees, and rose to her feet. The dirt on her palms felt warm from the sun as she offered him a small, respectful half-bow.

"I want to be alive at the end."

Rembran's answering smile was faint, almost wistful. "Life is rarely fair," he quoted, his tone half-playful, half-philosophical.

Rana blinked, caught between confusion and amusement, then shot him an exasperated look that made him chuckle.

"What?"

The raven-haired Hin I-Balanath tapped her foot, her eyes dancing with restrained laughter, and then a giggle escaped her. "That's what Maighstir Rhyslin keeps saying," she said, looking up at Rembran with a faint blush that colored her cheeks.

The elder spellblade's laughter rumbled like distant thunder, warm and unguarded. "Where do you think I heard that?" he said, grinning.

He waved over his shoulder, and through the dispersing crowd, Andros appeared, massive, patient, and grinning in that way only an elemental-bound could. The soldier carried Rana's sword carefully across his forearms, as though presenting a relic.

"Thank you." Rana took her sword and slid it back into its sheath with the comforting *shhkk* of steel on leather. She adjusted her belt and asked, "So, what's next?"

Rembran glanced around the field, his eyes falling on his fallen shield nearby. A soldier stooped to retrieve it and offered it back with a crisp nod. "Unless you care to try the duel again," he said, amusement tugging at the corner of his mouth, "we can go to the armory and see if we can find you either an arming sword or some kind of armor."

Rana's nose wrinkled at that. "I don't know if I want armor. I've learned to move fast without it." She pointed toward his mail shirt, the dull links gleaming faintly in the sun. "I don't want to encase myself in iron."

Rembran tilted his head, studying her as though reassessing a puzzle piece that had just shifted shape.

341

He stepped back, eyes sweeping over her attire. "Your skirts are leather, right?"

Rana nodded.

"And your boots?"

Another nod.

"Your blouse is what, heavy cotton or silk with heavy cotton underneath?"

Yet another nod.

"I wouldn't change a thing either," he said at last, approval softening his tone. "So, an arming sword or a dirk, I think."

Rana tilted her head down, thoughtful, her fingers brushing absently across her lips as she weighed the choice. "Yes, sir." Then she looked up, the spark of curiosity back in her hazel eyes. "I'm also going to train with Maighstir Tanner, correct?"

Rembran nodded. "Yes, I get to train you on odd days, Marcus on even days, and you don't get a break from Rhyslin."

He grinned, the lines at his eyes deepening with mischief. "You have him this afternoon."

Rana blinked. "Why?"

She couldn't quite hide the incredulity in her tone. Combat she understood; field tactics and wilderness training made sense. But Rhyslin's lessons? Those were something else.

The spellblade shrugged, adjusting the strap on his shoulder. "Rhyslin said something about teaching you how to access different branches of Draoidheachd."

Rana's expression lit up. For a heartbeat, she was all eagerness, the bright hunger of a student who lived for knowledge. She had wanted to learn that ever since Maighstir Eriand told her there were spells he could not touch. The idea that she might surpass even that barrier thrilled her.

In her mind's eye, possibilities began to unfurl, light, shadow, flame, and frost, all within reach.

She decided then and there that if she could, she'd ask Marcus to teach her how to use a short bow, too.

Rembran watched her quietly, his expression softening. He could almost see the ideas flickering behind her eyes like starlight. "The armory closes right before lunch and reopens two hours after lunch," he reminded her. "If we don't hurry, it'll be closed before you can get a second weapon."

"Oh," Rana said, blinking back to the moment. "Then let's go. If what you said is right, I must meet Maighstir Rhyslin after lunch." She brushed her hair over one shoulder, her dark braid catching the sunlight, and waited for him to lead the way.

Without another word between them, Rembran started across the field, his long strides cutting through the soft chatter of the other trainees. Rana followed, the grass whispering under her boots.

They passed a stand of old trees, their branches heavy with green leaves, and the scent of resin and dust hung in the warm air.

The path curved behind a cluster of barracks, where the faint clang of metal on metal began to echo. The rhythmic ringing grew louder as they neared a nondescript stone building half-hidden by the shade of the trees.

At the back, a narrow door stood open into a small courtyard, where the air shimmered with heat. The smell of charcoal, oil, and hot iron rolled out to meet them. Sparks occasionally flew from the doorway, flaring gold against the dim interior.

Rembran stepped forward, stuck his head through the open door, and called above the noise, "Telfort, are you busy?"

The hammering paused, followed by a voice thick with amusement. "Who wants to bloody know?"

Rembran turned to Rana and grinned theatrically, eyebrows raised, as if sharing a secret performance. "Who else would bother the renowned Telfort, Maighstir fear-ceairde of the Saorsa?" He swept into a grand, exaggerated bow, voice full of pompous flourish. "It is a humble spellblade that you know as Rembran."

A great belly laugh echoed from within, rolling out with the scent of smoke and iron. "Rembran, humble? Get your arse in here before I laugh myself to death!"

"Yes, Maighstir Telfort," Rembran said, laughing as he ducked through the doorway, the glow of the forge reflecting in his armor.

346

He reached back, hand extended, and pulled Rana inside after him.

The smithy was a cavern of heat and rhythm.

Inside, a tall, broad-shouldered man set his hammer aside on the anvil, where its head glowed faintly red in the forge-light. Sparks floated like fireflies in the haze, and the air was thick with the mingled scents of hot metal, oil, and old smoke. When he turned to look at the two spellblades entering his domain, his hazel eyes gleamed like burnished bronze.

Telfort was easily six feet tall, his short, wiry white hair damp with sweat, his arms corded with the strength of long habit. The forge-light painted his face in gold and shadow.

"Rembran, you irredeemable vagabond," he said, voice booming with familiar affection. "What brings you here, and who is this beautiful woman?"

Rembran spread his hands in mock offense, a grin curling at his lips. "Let me start with the introductions. Rana, this is Master Craftsman Ilion Telfort. Master Telfort, this is Rana, the daughter of one of Rhyslin's bannaichean."

Rana dipped into a graceful curtsey, her movement a soft counterpoint to the rough sounds of the forge. "Master Telfort, it is an honor to meet such an esteemed craftsman."

The smith returned her courtesy with surprising poise, bowing low in the heat-flickered light. His eyes, sharp despite his years, swept over her with the keen attention of one who weighed both steel and spirit.

"This is no mere *leanabh an fhàsaich*, I dare say. Just as her name is not truly Rana."

348

He studied her stance, the way her fingers rested lightly on the hilt at her side. "She carries herself with dignity and grace."

Rana offered a small, composed smile, the kind that warmed rather than invited. Telfort leaned in slightly, intrigued.

"Young lady, may I see your blade?"

Something in his tone, curiosity edged with reverence, told her he already suspected the truth. She drew her sword in a smooth motion, the steel singing softly as it left the sheath, and offered it to him hilt-first. The reflection of the forgefire raced down its length like liquid sunlight.

Telfort took the weapon carefully, almost ceremonially, holding it across both palms. His eyes flicked down the blade, drinking in every line and etching.

The hammer's glow gleamed off the metal, catching on the faint pattern that marked a master's touch.

"This is a *clach-iarainn* blade," he murmured, awe threading his voice. "And if my eyes don't deceive me, it was forged by Utar Penragun."

He turned the hilt slightly, showing the mark to Rembran.

Rana's lips curved faintly upward, pleased that he recognized it. "It was."

Telfort nodded, eyes bright. He turned the sword once more before handing it back to her, both hands steady and respectful.

"High-ranking Hin I-Balanath officers, Hin I-Balanath nobility, and the Royal Family carry Utar's weapons."

He studied her anew, as if seeing her for the first time.

"Rembran, my friend, do you realize this young lady is probably a Hin I-Balanath princess?"

Rembran's grin widened. "I do. Her mother is the former *banrigh fhàsach*, Ilyriatri. She is one of Rhyslin's *bannaichean*."

Telfort blinked, the revelation striking through his composure like a hammer blow. "I have never heard of such a thing." His gaze turned back to Rana, a mix of confusion and awe softening into respect. "What can I do for you?" He hesitated, his calloused hands twitching as if unsure what gesture suited royalty. "I'm not even sure how to address you."

Rana found herself liking this tall, blunt man, his honesty, his warmth, the way he met her eyes without hesitation.

"My mother is no longer queen, and I am no longer a princess," she said softly. The forgefire painted her face in shades of amber and rose. "I am now simply Rana."

And she meant it. There was peace in those words, freedom, even. For the first time since she'd come to Saorsa, she felt entirely at home in her own name.

"Rembran said you could find me or forge a short sword or dirk to use with my blade."

Telfort's answering grin was bright and immediate. "Follow me, simply Rana." He swept one broad arm toward the forge's side chamber, where rows of weapons gleamed under the lamplight. "Let's see if we can find you a short sword that will complement Utar's blade."

Rana accepted his invitation, her boots whispering over the stone floor as she followed him. The air grew warmer as they stepped into the armory, where every wall was a gallery of steel, swords, axes, daggers, and spears, each meticulously crafted and lovingly displayed.

Her hazel eyes flitted from blade to blade, catching on the subtle curve of a pommel here, the etched line of a fuller there. The rhythmic hiss of the forge carried faintly through the doorway, like a giant's breath.

Telfort leaned back against the doorjamb, arms folded, watching her. There was a craftsman's appreciation in his gaze, not the gaze of a man admiring beauty for its own sake, but of someone recognizing poise and curiosity in equal measure.

Rana bent to examine a short sword, its blade catching the orange glow as she tested its balance. With practiced grace, she extended it before her, gauging the weight, then handed it to Rembran to hold.

Fifteen minutes passed in that steady rhythm, the clink of steel, the soft shuffle of boots, the low murmur of appraisal.

Two short swords, a dirk, and a dagger later, Rana stood once again in the courtyard, testing the last of them under the open light.

When she made her choice, she turned toward the smith. "I like this one. It's almost the right size." She handed him the thirteen-inch dirk, her tone matter-of-fact but eyes glinting with satisfaction. "Do you have one that's about an inch shorter?"

For the first time since entering the forge, mischief sparked in her expression. She batted her eyes at Telfort, playful and utterly at ease.

The smith laughed under his breath, shaking his head fondly as he crossed to a rack of blades. His heavy fingers brushed along the hilts one by one, tapping, testing, until he stopped halfway down. "Here you go, *bhean bheag*," he said, lifting a slimmer dirk from its place.

Rana smiled inwardly as she accepted the weapon, another nickname, another thread in the web of belonging she was slowly weaving here. With quiet dignity, she fastened the sheath to the right side of her belt, the metal buckle snapping into place. She bowed her head slightly, voice soft but firm.

"Thank you, Maighstir Telfort. I will always treat this blade with honor."

"Ah, lass, may it keep you alive," he replied, warmth threading through the gruffness. His eyes gleamed in the firelight. "What's next?"

The forge crackled, and for a moment, time seemed to hold still, the air full of heat, steel, and promise. Rana touched the new dirk at her side, feeling its perfect weight, and smiled.

Whatever came next, she was ready.

Chapter Seventeen
The Law of the Gods

The heat of the forge had softened into a comfortable warmth that clung to the air like a lingering breath. Sunlight slanted across the courtyard, striking firelight glints from the blades hung on the walls. The smell of hot iron, oil, and leather mingled with the faint sweetness of sawdust from the carpenter's stalls beyond.

Rana sat on the low edge of the anvil's base, tapping her fingers absently on the hilt of her new dirk as she thought about the rest of her day.

"Four *uairean* of lessons with *maighstir* Rhyslin."

Telfort raised a brow as he quenched a fresh-forged hinge in a trough of water.

The hiss filled the pause before his question. "Doing what?"

Rana shrugged, a bright grin tugging at the corners of her mouth. "Studying *Draoidheachd*, I guess." She let the word roll musically off her tongue. "Or healing, or maybe history."

The smith's eyes twinkled as he looked toward Rembran, who leaned against the doorframe, arms crossed, one boot braced casually behind him. The spellblade shrugged. "I've never seen anyone so happy to have to sit through healing or history classes."

Rana laughed, a clear, ringing sound that seemed to brighten the air. "You wouldn't understand. Any time with *mo aon socair* is time well spent."

Both men exchanged a knowing glance over her head.

"Me thinks *a' bhean bheag* is in love," Telfort quipped.

357

Rana threw her head back in mock disinterest, a theatrical roll of her eyes. "Put two men together; they'll think a woman is in love," she teased, voice lilting with humor.

Rembran chuckled. "She didn't deny it."

"Why would I deny it?" Rana crowed. "He's helping me learn to survive."

"Aye, lass, that he is," Telfort said matter-of-factly. "That's what he does. That's what he always does."

The smile faded a little from her lips as she turned toward Rembran and met his eyes. Her tone shifted—gentler, quieter, more vulnerable.

"Do you know what it's like to be ignored by every adult in my village?" She glanced at Telfort, the forge glow softening the intensity of her expression. "Or be looked down on or humored?"

When neither man answered, she blushed faintly and looked down. "*Maighstir* Rhyslin has never treated me like a child. He's treated me like a woman, and—" her voice softened until it was almost a whisper, "I love him."

The last words came like a confession slipping through her defenses, and for a heartbeat, the forge seemed to hold its breath.

Rembran only nodded, the faintest flicker of knowing in his eyes. He had suspected it, but the weight of hearing it aloud made him glance away, thoughtful.

Rana's gaze dropped to the dusty stones at her feet. "He's still figuring out how he feels about Momma and Flur. It's okay that he's not sure about me." Her blush deepened. "I might not even survive my doom," she whispered. "I will be happy while I can."

Both men froze at the quiet fatalism in her tone. They started to reach out, Rembran a steadying hand, Telfort a fatherly gesture, but Rana danced lightly back out of reach, smiling again.

"You can't change my doom any more than I can," she said warmly. "And I appreciate you caring for me."

The forge light caught in her hair as she straightened, looking between them with genuine curiosity.

"Can I ask you guys a question?"

When they nodded, she sank against the side of the anvil, drawing her knees up and resting her chin atop them. Her tone was pensive now, her earlier laughter folded into thought.

"What makes you guys different from every man I've ever met?"

Rembran's brow quirked. "What do you mean?"

"You treat your women like women. You treat us like we want to be treated, and you don't pamper us." She lifted one hand, counting softly on her fingers. "Rhyslin treats Flur like she wants to be treated. He treats Momma like she wants. He treats Rowena like she wants. And he treats me like I want to be treated."

She pointed to Rembran. "You seem to know what Ixa wants and treat her appropriately." Her eyes narrowed slightly in wonder. "Why?"

Rembran smiled faintly, then placed a calloused hand gently atop hers. "I always blame the gods. They've dabbled so much, especially Ananke and Chantico, that we understand what women want."

Rana tilted her head, curiosity sparking again. "So, it's just here, in the *Saorsa*?"

Rembran chuckled, leaning back with an easy grace. "It wouldn't surprise me."

He tapped his fingers on his thigh in thought. "They are very closed mouthed about where they have followers. We don't know what's happening in the old empire."

"I see." Rana nodded slowly, considering that. "So, it's the gods' fault?"

The smith laughed softly, the sound rumbling deep in his chest. "Living in the *Saorsa* made it easy to follow the teachings." He sighed, setting down his hammer. "That and we do love our women."

Rana leaned forward, resting her forearms on her knees. "What keeps a man from forcing a woman to bond with him?"

The question hit like a spark in dry tinder. Both men exchanged a loaded look.

"Ananke."

Rana's eyes narrowed; she clearly wanted more than that.

Rembran sighed, rubbing the back of his neck. "We really can't explain it how you want us to."

"This is more of a *draoidh* type question," Telfort admitted. "This goes beyond feelings; it involves things that hurt my head." He gave her a sheepish grin. "Maybe you should ask Rhyslin. He can probably explain it better."

Rana exhaled in quiet frustration. "If you say so." She pushed herself upright, brushing her hands off on her skirt, and bowed her head to the smith. "Thank you, *Maighstir* Telfort."

When he nodded acknowledgment, she turned toward the courtyard door. "I guess it's time to find *Maighstir* Rhyslin. Can you show me how to get out of here, Rembran?"

"Sure." The spellblade fell into step beside her.

They walked out through the alleyways, past the drying lines of leather and the echo of distant hammering, until the practice fields opened ahead like a sunlit meadow.

"Can you find your way back from here?" Rembran asked.

"I can," Rana said, smiling sidelong at him. "I think you are trying to get rid of me."

Oh, my goddess, I'm teasing him again, she realized, feeling the warmth of amusement rise in her cheeks.

"Of course I am," Rembran admitted with mock gravity. "You're taking away from my time with Ixa."

Rana froze mid-step and turned toward him, studying his face. There was no meanness in his tone, only gentle humor. A slow, knowing smile curved her lips.

"It's too bad that we must go to the same place to spend time with Ixa. Maybe you should get your own place."

Rembran laughed, a deep, genuine sound. "I have my own place, and you know it. If you hadn't taken time to have tea and cookies with Ananke and Despoina, we could have gone home last night."

"*Touché*," she replied with a grin, bowing her head in mock defeat.

They traded banter all the way up the path until they reached the wide stone steps of the mansion. The afternoon light washed them in gold, soft and forgiving.

"Thank you for walking me back," Rana said graciously, turning to face him. "Go find Ixa and spend some time with her." She made a shooing gesture with both hands.

"You're welcome, *piuthar bheag*," Rembran replied, his voice touched with unmistakable affection.

Rana stopped short, the words sinking in. *Little sister.*

The phrase settled warmly in her chest, deeper than she expected. Her blush returned, faint but radiant, and she bowed her head slightly, glancing up at him from beneath her lashes. He wasn't mocking her, he meant it.

The realization filled her with a giddy, childlike joy. She turned, her braid swinging, and skipped up the stairs, humming softly to herself as the door closed behind her.

Rana found *Maighstir* Rhyslin waiting in the broad, sun-warmed study that adjoined the library. The scent of parchment, wax, and old ink filled the air, softened by the faint aroma of dried herbs from the alchemical table near the window. Afternoon light poured through tall mullioned glass, painting golden bars across shelves of tomes and scrolls.

"Good afternoon, *Aon Socair*," she greeted as she stepped across the threshold.

"Good afternoon, *mo phrìseil*," he returned warmly, looking up from the open book before him. His quill rested neatly to one side, the faintest smile curving his lips as he marked his place with a ribbon.

Rana leaned against the desk, palms pressed to its smooth surface, the warmth of the sunlit wood beneath her skin. "What do you plan to teach me?"

He slid the book closed and gestured toward the couch before the hearth. "*Draoidheachd*, healing, history." His tone was calm, measured, yet inviting. "What would you like to learn today?"

She sank onto the couch, nibbling at her lower lip, her thoughts whirling. The question that had haunted her since the forge still burned behind her teeth. She hesitated, uncertain how he would take it.

Rhyslin's gaze softened. "What's wrong, Rana?"

Her pulse jumped. *To ifrinn with it,* she muttered under her breath, deciding to face it head-on. She shifted, making herself comfortable before speaking aloud. "I asked *Maighstirs* Telfort and Rembran a question they couldn't answer."

He leaned back slightly, one eyebrow raised, inviting her to continue.

"What keeps a man from forcing a woman to bond with him?"

The room stilled, the sounds of the world outside, pages turning in the distant library, a soft wind brushing the windowpanes, fading into silence.

Rhyslin drew a long, steadying breath, then exhaled slowly. "You don't ask the easy questions, do you?"

"I'm sorry, *Maighstir Rhyslin,*" Rana murmured, her gaze dropping to the polished floor.

He almost told her not to apologize, but something in her tone stopped him. She *meant* it, not as guilt, but respect. "There's nothing to be sorry about, Rana."

He paused, searching for the right way to bridge mystery and understanding. "Do you know how bonds work? Do you know how they are created?"

When she shook her head, he closed his eyes briefly, centering himself. The afternoon light caught in the silver strands of his hair. "I will try to explain it as I see it, as I have experienced it."

He folded his hands loosely in his lap, his voice quiet but resonant, like a prayer spoken in confidence. "Being bonded means more than just two people meeting each other and falling in love."

Rana leaned forward slightly, her eyes intent.

"The creation of a bond is beyond the mere feelings of love. It's the sharing of two souls. There is no way to hide in a bond." His gaze drifted toward the hearth, the firelight flickering across his features. "I can't lie to those I'm bonded with; the bond won't let me."

He looked back at her, the air between them dense with unspoken reverence. "A bond requires two or more people to know each other on a deeply personal level. A man trying to force a woman to bond with him would have to first open himself completely to her, allowing her to see his soul. He would have to admit to her that he wants to enslave her, and he would have to force her to lie to Ananke and force her to acknowledge the bond, which she will never do."

Rana's lips parted; her mouth had gone dry. "Has it ever been tried?"

"Sadly, yes," Rhyslin admitted. His eyes dimmed with memory. "Men and women have tried to force a bond."

"What happened to them?"

"Ananke refused to honor it," he said solemnly. "The people trying to force the bond were killed by the gods and, in some cases, torn from the wheel and thrown into the outer darkness."

A shiver coursed through her. "That sounds so final."

"It is, *mo phriseil,* it is."

Rana released a long sigh, her shoulders easing as the weight of fear began to lift. The knowledge brought unexpected comfort.

Rhyslin noticed the way her posture softened and tilted his head. "How do you feel about it?"

"I'm relieved, for some reason," she admitted, sinking deeper into the couch cushions.

"It means that whatever will happen to me, at least I can't be forced to bind with someone, unless Meron is around." She said, remembering what the Magus had done to Ixa and Andros.

Her eyes flicked back to him, curiosity sparking again. *I wonder how deep a bond goes.* "*Maighstir Rhyslin.* Can you tell what Momma is thinking?"

Rhyslin's expression gentled. He hummed softly as he reclined in his chair. "Let's see."

He closed his eyes, and the stillness around him seemed to shift—subtle but palpable. The golden light in the room dimmed against the weight of his focus.

"She's worried about you, but that's a given." His voice lowered, more resonant now, as if reaching beyond the visible world. "You're never very far from her thoughts."

He opened his eyes, watching the emotions ripple across Rana's face, first tenderness, then gratitude, then peace.

"Now," he continued, smiling faintly, "she's trying to figure out how you are doing."

When Rana raised an eyebrow in quiet challenge, he added, "She's satisfied to know you are fine."

Rana laughed softly, a sound like wind through leaves. "That sounds like Momma," she said, the happiness in her tone unmistakable. "I used to think that she was a worrywart. But, since coming here, I know differently."

She slid forward, her knees nearly touching his, and reached out to rest her hand gently on his. "Thank you, *mo Aon Socair*."

Rhyslin turned his hand, cupping hers between his palms. "You are welcome, *mo phriseil.*"

The room seemed to breathe again, the quiet creak of wood, the faint song of birds from the courtyard window.

Rana brushed her free hand through her hair, her smile returning. "So, *Maighstir Marcus?*"

Rhyslin nodded, lips curving in amusement.

"What will I be learning?" she asked, her tone bright with anticipation.

"Knowing Marcus, woodland survival, tracking, hunting." His eyes gleamed. "Also, knowing Marcus, he'll pair you with his daughter, and she ... well, she will be undergoing her trials," he paused, a half-smile ghosting across his mouth. "And she's going to be better than you. Don't lose your patience."

Rana blushed, her cheeks warming to a soft rose hue. She bowed her head slightly, eyes glinting with a mixture of humility and resolve. "Yes, *Maighstir Rhyslin.*"

Outside, the sun had begun its descent, casting long amber rays through the study windows. The air shimmered with dust motes that glowed like tiny constellations.

In the hush that followed, the faint warmth of divine presence seemed to linger, the echo of Ananke's unseen hand, the quiet thread of truth that bound them all.

Chapter Eighteen
The Call Beyond the Stone

The late afternoon light slanted through the tall windows of Rhyslin's study, burnishing the polished mahogany of his desk and the brass fittings of the lamps. The faint scent of oil and parchment hung in the still air. Books lined the walls from floor to ceiling, their leather spines gleaming like dark jewels. Somewhere deeper in the house, a clock chimed softly, a reminder of the unhurried rhythm that governed this place.

"*Maighstir,*" said Kenna, the cat girl whose blond locks bobbed in time with her steps. Her soft leather slippers barely made a sound on the tiled floor. Her ears were turned in his direction, and her tail swayed lazily from side to side in a languid rhythm that matched her voice.

Rhyslin looked up from his desk, the tip of his quill still wet with ink. "What is it, Kenna?" His tone was calm and even, the measured cadence of a man accustomed to bearing news both great and grim.

Encouraged by his lack of irritation, Kenna flounced over to him, an envelope clasped delicately between her fingers. The sunlight caught in her golden hair and the fine fur of her ears, giving her a faint, haloed glow.

She purred as she handed him the envelope. "It's from the council, *Maighstir*. I signed for it." Her tail flicked with satisfaction, and she stood a little straighter, obviously proud. Reading and writing were her treasures, and signing her name in elegant, looping script was her small rebellion against the world that once dismissed her kind.

Rhyslin accepted the envelope, weighing it thoughtfully in his left hand. "It's about time." The vellum was thick and heavy, sealed in deep green wax stamped with the Council's sigil.

When the cat-girl tilted her head in curiosity, one ear twitching, Rhyslin continued, "It should be about the hin I-Balanath treaties."

Kenna's ears flattened slightly as she counted on her fingers. "Did you notify them of the treaties five weeks ago?"

Rhyslin nodded, the faintest sigh escaping him. "Yes. I suppose the *An fheadhainn a thuit* raids kept them busy for a few weeks." He tapped the envelope against the desk, then slid open the top drawer, retrieving a slender silver letter opener. Its blade gleamed in the dim light as he sliced neatly through the seal.

The soft *crack* of wax breaking sounded loud in the quiet room. He drew out the folded vellum, its scent faintly of iron gall ink and candle smoke, and smoothed it flat upon the desktop. The sound of the parchment unfolding echoed like a whisper of old authority.

He read aloud:

Rhyslin Darkblade, am flur mansa

Maighstir Darkblade, the council wishes to notify you that we have finally dulled the orcan / an fheadhainn a thuit threat enough for a council meeting.

One of the topics on the agenda will be the hin i-balanath treaties.

It has been brought to our attention that one of the hin i-balanath banrig's has since become your banniachean.

For her people to have representation, she must select a hin i-balanath male to represent them at the council meeting, which will be held in seven (7) days in Austown.

Conrad Vogelsang — current head of the saorsa council.

✳︎◦–◇–◦✳︎

Rhyslin's brows lifted slightly. He read it again, slower this time, letting the meaning settle like sediment in a glass of water. Then, with a soft hum, he slid the letter opener back into the drawer, its metallic click punctuating his thoughts.

"Kenna, can you do me a favor?"

The cat-girl's eyes brightened, her tail swishing in a slow S-shaped pattern. "Do I get a head-pat out of it?" she purred, her grin mischievous, one fang catching the light.

Rhyslin laughed, the sound low and genuine, echoing softly through the study. "Of course."

He reached up and scratched her gently between the ears. Her loud, contented purr filled the air like a vibration of joy, her tail curling in delight.

"Would you be a dear and go get Ria for me?"

"I will, I will." She kneaded her hands on his shoulders in an affectionate little gesture before bounding toward the door.

Her footsteps faded into the hall, followed by the faintest hum of her voice, a contented melody that blended with the creak of old timbers.

Rhyslin returned his gaze to the letter, his eyes narrowing slightly. The council's words seemed to ripple with implication. Outside the windows, a breeze stirred, carrying the faint rustle of leaves and the scent of rain yet to fall.

It took less than five minutes for Ria to arrive, either Kenna had sprinted the entire distance or Ria had been near at hand. The door opened softly, and the dark-haired bhanna entered, the faint sound of her bare feet whispering against the floor.

"Kenna said that you wanted to see me," she said, brushing a stray lock of raven hair behind her left ear.

The gesture was simple, but her poise carried the quiet authority of one who had once worn a crown.

Rhyslin nodded and gestured to the couch beside his desk. The cushions sank slightly as she sat, crossing one leg gracefully over the other.

"This came from the council," he said, tapping the letter where it lay upon the polished wood. "The treaties that we brokered are set to be confirmed. However, there is one tiny problem."

Ria chuckled, her smile teasing yet sharp. "That would be me being your *bhanna* instead of a *banrìgh,* wouldn't it?"

"That's right." He studied her expression, tracing every subtle flicker of amusement and resignation. "This council you mentioned, who is in charge?"

Her lips curved into a smirk. "Are you getting senile in your old age?" she teased, her eyes gleaming. "We've been over this already."

Rhyslin rolled his eyes and sighed with mock gravity. "You know how it is once you pass six hundred. The mind is the first thing to go."

Ria's laughter filled the study, bright and warm. It softened the air, driving away the faint tension left by the council's decree.

"Makar Lann Neimh is, was my first minister," she said at last.

"He's probably already called another council meeting, and it wouldn't surprise me if he shows up within the next day or so."

"That soon?" Rhyslin's tone sharpened with interest. "Will they be able to open a portal?"

Ria nodded, her expression wry. "*A' Mathair* has set secret portals for us to use. It wouldn't surprise me if he hasn't already begged her for power." She leaned toward him slightly, eyes glittering with mischief. "I hope you're ready to defend yourself, for I'll wager the first thing he does is call you out for keeping me away from home."

A wry grin curved Rhyslin's mouth. "I could just give you back to him."

Ria's eyes widened, her voice softening into a whisper. "Don't you dare, *mo maighstir gràdh.*" She rose from the couch, the movement smooth and feline, and pushed him gently back from his desk before climbing into his lap. Her warmth pressed close to him as she looked up with a defiant glint. "You wouldn't, would you?"

"I would never dream of it," the *draoidh* murmured, his hand finding the small of her back in a gesture both protective and possessive.

"Good, I'm your Ria until I die," she whispered, burying her face beneath his chin. Her voice softened into a purr, half challenge, half vow. "And when we all die, I will find a way to be your *bhanna* again and again."

"*Mathair* willing," Rhyslin breathed, his fingers catching in her dark hair as he tilted her head up to kiss her, deep, reverent, and unhurried. The air between them shimmered with the quiet hum of shared magic.

"Did you send a missive to Makar before we left the Three Rivers fort?"

Ria nodded, her cheek still pressed to his collar. "I did. He should have gotten it a week ago." She smiled against him. "I'll bet he gathered the council and immediately informed them of his plans." A soft moan escaped her as his fingers trailed down her back. "You're going to be in trouble," she sang, her voice lilting as she looked up into his eyes.

"Did you tell Makar that you'd bonded with me?" Rhyslin's tone was mild, but there was curiosity beneath it.

Ria blinked, and then realization dawned. Her eyes widened. "No, because we hadn't bonded then," she admitted, blushing faintly. Thoughts flickered behind her eyes, the teasing, the ceremony, the weight of the vow. "Rhyslin, you wouldn't give me up, would you?"

"It would break my heart to do so," Rhyslin said softly. "I love you. You've become a part of my heart." He leaned his forehead against hers. "Would you be willing to do something for me?"

"Of course, I would." She batted her lashes playfully. "What would you like me to do?"

"To talk to Makar and bring him back," Rhyslin said, brushing his fingers along her jaw.

She nuzzled into his palm, her purr a quiet vibration. "You know I'll go." Then, with a sly grin, she added, "I could bring back more than him."

"You could," he agreed, his smile small but knowing, "but you won't." His eyes searched hers, steady and kind. "I'll leave how many you bring up to you."

He sighed softly. "I should also send Flur to talk to her mother."

Ria arched a single dark eyebrow. "Trying to cover everything important?"

Rhyslin tapped the letter. "The council found out before I could tell them, so yes. I think that covering everything important is the way to go."

Ria leaned forward, her voice softening until it was almost a sigh. "Yes, *maighstir*. I will go."

Outside, the first drops of rain began to patter softly against the glass. The study's lamps flickered, their light golden and warm, casting the two of them in the glow of a world poised between love and obligation.

The library was aglow with lamplight, golden reflections dancing off polished oak shelves and the gilt lettering of hundreds of ancient tomes.

A faint scent of parchment, candle wax, and woodsmoke hung in the air, the comforting perfume of Rhyslin's home. Outside, dusk had settled, staining the tall windows with indigo shadows while rain whispered softly against the panes.

Flur's voice broke the quiet like a breeze through curtains.

"What are you two up to?" she inquired with a playful grin as Rhyslin and Ria walked into the library, hand in hand.

The couple's silence spoke more than words. Their fingers remained entwined as they crossed the threshold. The warmth of the hearth glinted on Ria's dark hair and touched the faint silver in Rhyslin's white locks.

When neither answered her, Flur leaned forward in her chair, her grin fading into curiosity. "What's up?"

Rhyslin settled onto the couch, the leather creaking softly beneath him. He waited for Ria to sit beside him before sliding an arm around her shoulders. The movement was small, instinctive, yet carried the weight of unspoken affection.

Flur looked from one to the other, her voice dropping. "Maighstir, Ria. You're starting to worry me." She paled slightly. "Am I in trouble?"

"No, it's nothing like that." Rhyslin reached out and pulled Flur onto the couch on his other side. The scent of her floral perfume, light and clean, mingled with the warm musk of the room. "Ria is going to take a trip for me."

The blond-haired *Hin I-Balanath* snuggled close, her cheek brushing against his shoulder, and murmured, "Where's she going?"

"I'm going to the manor to talk to my first minister," Ria said softly, her tone steady but tinged with melancholy. "The council somehow learned about my bond with Rhyslin, and Makar will have to sign the treaty in my place."

Flur inhaled sharply, her breath catching in the hush between them. "Do you need me to do anything?" She gazed at him with the bluest of eyes, wide, earnest, and impossibly trusting.

"How would you like to visit your mother and see if she and Maya can be here in a week?"

Flur's eyes brightened instantly. Her smile bloomed, pure and golden. "Of course, I can, Maighstir." She winked. "When do we leave?"

Rhyslin sighed softly, his voice dropping into the mellow timbre that made even orders sound like kindness.

"There's no time like the present," he said as he relaxed slightly into the couch. "The sooner you both leave, the sooner you can get back."

Flur and Ria exchanged a glance, some private mirth dancing between them. Then Flur leaned back with a teasing glimmer in her eye. "It sounds like you are going to miss us."

"I will," Rhyslin admitted, the truth landing like a quiet confession. "Both of you have become parts of my life. I will miss you every second you are gone."

That admission earned him soft "awwws" from both women, followed by affectionate snuggles and kisses that filled the air with laughter and warmth.

"That's so sweet," Flur cooed, batting her eyelashes dramatically.

"It's not surprising," Ria said, her voice soft and low as velvet. "Our beloved *maighstir* has a deep and complex heart." She placed a kiss on his right cheek, her lips cool and sure, and Flur immediately mirrored her on the left.

"Give us a few *mionaidean,* and we'll be right back."

The two women rose together, their skirts brushing the floor, and left the room in a flurry of light steps and faint perfume.

As they vanished down the corridor, their laughter trailed faintly behind them, mingling with the low hiss of rain outside.

Rhyslin turned toward the door just as it creaked open again. Rana stepped in, her dark braid damp from the mist outside, her expression curious.

"What's momma getting ready for?"

The *draoidh* gestured to the couch, his hand making a slow, deliberate sweep. The firelight threw gentle shadows across his features as he watched her cross the room. She sat gracefully, smoothing her skirt before folding her hands in her lap, patient, composed.

"Ria is taking a short trip back to *Comraich uisge na gealaich*," he explained. His tone carried both weight and warmth.

To her credit, the young spell-blade didn't interrupt but waited, her hazel eyes steady. It earned her a small nod of approval.

"The *Saorsa* Council will meet in seven days and discuss the treaties with the *Hin I-Balanath*."

When Rana arched an eyebrow, he shook his head slightly, amused at her restraint.

"Your mother, being *bhanna,* cannot represent your people and needs a council member to replace her. She's going to go get Makar."

She nodded her understanding, fingers tapping once against her knee before she asked, "Do you want to go with her or stay here?"

Rana lifted her hand and cupped her chin in thought. Her eyes drifted toward the rain-smeared windows, toward a world that once meant home but now only felt distant. The manor had lost its hold on her the moment she began calling this place *hers.*

She shook her head softly, a faint smile curving her lips. "I want to stay here and continue my training."

Her gaze lifted to meet his. "I have to attend training with Maighstir Marcus tomorrow, right?"

"Indeed you do," Rhyslin replied, the corners of his mouth twitching in faint amusement. "And you'll have to start early to get there by the eighth hour."

He leaned back slightly, studying her. "He lives several leagues from here, and your first test will be to find his hunting shack."

Rana frowned, her brows knitting adorably as she tilted her head. "Is there a map?"

When he nodded, she smiled sweetly, her eyes dancing. "May I see it, please, Maighstir?"

Rhyslin sighed, brushing his fingers through his white hair in mock exasperation. "Of course. How else are you going to find the shack?"

Before he could move, Rana sprang up and, with an agility born of training and youth, crawled into his lap.

"Thank you, Maighstir," she whispered, her voice small and soft against the quiet patter of rain. She nestled against him, her head finding its place on his shoulder. The warmth of her breath brushed his neck; her hair smelled faintly of soap and night air.

A tender smile crossed his lips. He lifted one hand and began to trace gentle circles down her back, a habit as natural as breathing.

"You'll need to get to bed early tonight," he murmured. "The fourth hour is going to come early."

Instead of answering, Rana purred faintly, the sound low and rhythmic, the kind of sound that vibrated in the chest rather than the air. She melted under his touch, her body softening in contentment.

After a few minutes, she grinned sleepily against his shoulder. "If you keep this up, you'll have to carry me to bed."

"Perish the thought," Rhyslin said, and she gave a little huff of mock annoyance.

"If you don't want to, you don't have to," she mumbled, trying to pull away half-heartedly.

Instead of letting her go, he continued his slow caress, his fingers tracing the line of her spine. "I never said that I didn't want to," he whispered into the raven locks on her head.

"You're mean," Rana murmured, her voice dissolving into a yawn. "But you're very good with your fingers."

A quiet chuckle escaped him, and within moments her breathing deepened. The girl was asleep, her small frame rising and falling gently against his chest.

Rhyslin shifted carefully, lifting her with practiced grace and laying her on the couch.

He drew a blanket over her shoulders, one embroidered in pale blue thread, soft from many years of use. For a moment, he just watched her sleep. The firelight painted her face in shades of gold and shadow, peaceful and young.

Two sets of footsteps sounded from the hallway, soft and measured. Ria and Flur appeared in the doorway, cloaked and ready. Their expressions were warm but tinged with that quiet melancholy that always comes before parting.

[*We are ready,*] Ria's voice brushed gently through the bond, her thought like a cool wind. [*Is she asleep?*]

Rhyslin nodded, rising from his chair. The movement stirred the room's stillness.

He looked down once more at the sleeping girl, then turned toward his bhanna and his golden-haired companion.

"Let's go," he whispered, his voice low but steady. "The portal stone is in the garden."

The lamps flickered as they turned to leave, and the faint scent of rain-wet air drifted in from the hall. Behind them, the fire hissed softly, the last sound of home before the night swallowed the light.

The garden lay cloaked in twilight. Silver light from a crescent moon traced the edges of ancient hedges and scattered across the moss-dappled stones beneath Rhyslin's feet. The air hummed faintly, alive with the scent of damp earth and faint ozone, the mark of old magic waiting to be stirred.

Fireflies drifted lazily among the ivy as if answering some invisible rhythm.

400

In the center of the garden stood the portal stone, a ring of smooth obsidian etched with runes that pulsed faintly with blue-white light, like stars awakening beneath the surface. Mist coiled around the base of the stone, carrying the faint tang of sea salt from the distant coast.

Ria stood within the circle, her cloak brushing against the faintly glowing symbols. Her dark hair shimmered where the moonlight touched it, and her hazel eyes glowed with equal parts courage and trepidation.

"How does this work?" Ria asked as she stood in the center of the portal stone. She had never traveled alone through a portal and had gotten used to having a mage travel with her.

Like her daughter's, her hazel eyes sparkled in the dim light as she gazed at Rhyslin. Even though she was nervous, she tried to hide it.

"It's just like any other portal," Rhyslin explained. "I activate it, it opens, and all you have to do is think of where you need to be."

"Need?" She queried with a raised eyebrow. "Not where I want to be?" Her lips turned up in a teasing smile.

"Shh," he reached out and cupped her right cheek, feeling her purr. "If you think of what you want, you won't go anywhere."

Her skin was warm beneath his hand, the faint vibration of her purr thrumming against his palm. The night air smelled faintly of rain and crushed mint.

"True," she whispered. "I don't want to be anywhere else but here, with you." Ria turned her head and kissed his palm, tasting the saltiness of his sweat.

"Um-hm," he replied. "But you need to go get Makar. When you have found him, you can come back."

"If he lets me," Ria said sadly. "He might decide to make me stay." She looked up into his eyes. "Then you'd have to come get me."

Rhyslin shook his head, a wry smile flickering beneath the lamplight. "Such drama. I don't think he'd appreciate it if I came to get you." He kissed her softly, drawing a moan from deep within her. "The quicker you leave, the quicker you can get back."

The air around them shimmered faintly as the portal stone began to respond to Rhyslin's gathering power. Runes along its edge flared to life, their light rippling outward like ripples on still water. A hush fell over the garden; even the insects paused.

Ria sighed as she disentangled herself from him. "You're right." She grasped his hand. "I'll miss you." Then, she let go of him. "Whenever you are ready, *mo ghràidh.*"

Rhyslin nodded and stepped back, the hem of his cloak brushing over the glowing runes. He traced a rune in the air with two fingers, the movement slow, deliberate, as if each curve were a prayer. A shimmer of blue fire followed the motion, hanging for a heartbeat before falling toward the stone. The circle blazed.

The darkness enveloped her, but it was not an empty dark. It pulsed with light, deep violet and cobalt hues twisting together, forming a tunnel of shadow and luminescence. Ria closed her eyes, picturing the manor house on the edge of a desert oasis, its white spires glinting under the sun, palm trees swaying in golden heat.

A low hum rose around her, then faded. The scent of roses and ozone mingled one last time before she vanished completely.

The *draoidh* watched as his second *bannaichean* disappeared into the shadows, the last trace of her presence lingering as warmth in the air. The runes dimmed but did not die; they pulsed faintly, waiting. Rhyslin exhaled slowly, his breath fogging in the chill night.

He turned to his first. "It's your turn, Flur."

The blond-haired *bhanna* stepped forward, her golden hair glinting like sunlight caught in moonlight. She gave him a dazzling smile as she stepped into the center of the stone. Her excitement crackled like static in the air.

"I have no idea where *Mathair* would be," she admitted. "She could be anywhere, from the manor house to Aunt Maya's."

She gazed into Rhyslin's eyes. "How do I find her?"

"Ah," Rhyslin vocalized. "In your case, you need to find your mother. Picture her, her face, her hair, her smile."

The air between them thickened with quiet intensity. He gathered Flur in a kiss that seared her soul, bright, tender, and electric with parting energy. The runes flared brighter for a heartbeat, mirroring the passion in the air.

"Do that, and you'll find her."

Flur waved her hand across her face, trying to hide a tear that glittered in the portal light. "Yes, *maighstir*." She hugged him before gathering herself and picturing Allanagh's face. "I'm ready."

After releasing her, Rhyslin reached into his robe and produced a crystal about the size of her palm, its facets shimmering with inner light.

He handed it to her; it was cool and heavy, etched with a spiral rune that pulsed faintly in rhythm with her heartbeat.

She looked at the object and raised an eyebrow. "What is this?"

"It's your way home," the *draoidh* said. "It's a mind stone. When you are ready to return, hold it and think of me. We'll be able to communicate."

The golden-haired bondswoman gazed at it before sliding it into a pocket on her skirt. "Why didn't Ria get one?"

Rhyslin shrugged, the gesture simple but fond. "Because she'll be back before you will. Since you don't know where you are going, I may need to cast a travel spell to get you back."

Flur nodded, her expression softening. She winked, her usual brightness returning. The faint light of the runes reflected in her eyes as she gathered her thoughts.

Rhyslin gave her another second, just long enough for the wind to stir, whispering through the garden leaves, before he redrew the rune. The circle flared once more, brighter than before.

The glow rose around her, swallowing her in spiraling strands of silver and gold. She laughed softly, her voice echoing in the magical hum. Then, in a flash of light and the scent of wildflowers, she was gone.

The night settled back into stillness. The portal stone's light faded to a low, pulsing heartbeat beneath the moss. Rhyslin stood alone in the garden, his robes stirring gently in the breeze, the taste of ozone and goodbye still clinging to the air.

He closed his eyes, feeling the faint tug of the bonds that stretched now across distance and dimension, threads of love and loyalty woven into the fabric of magic itself.

When he finally opened them, the moonlight caught the faintest shimmer of tears along his lashes.

Let's Keep in Touch (and in Tales)

I hope you enjoyed reading this book as much as I did writing it.

If you wish to read other books I've written, you will find them, in order, below.

The Draoidh's Cearcall (Series)

1—The Draoidh's Cearcall

2 — The Draoidh's Gambit

Forthcoming

3 — The Draoidh's Accord

4 — Shadows Rise

5 —The Draoidh's Fall

The Law Keeper Chronicles (Series)

1 — The Black Swan's Bond

Forthcoming

2 — The Sheriff's Oath

3 — By Law and Flame

The Web-Weaver's War (Series)

Forthcoming

1 — Oath & Ember

If you want to tag along for the fun, join my mailing list at:

https://josephwiess.substack.com/

www.ingramcontent.com/pod-product-compliance
Lightning Source LLC
Chambersburg PA
CBHW020541120726
47903CB00001B/78